MW01141162

A SKY BLACK
WITH CROWS

A SKY BLACK WITH CROWS

Alice Walsh

Red Deer PRESS

Copyright © 2006 Alice Walsh
Published in the United States in 2006
5 4 3 2 1

All rights reserved. No part of this publication may be reproduced, stored in a
retrieval system or transmitted, in any form or by any means, without the
prior written permission of Red Deer Press or, in case of photocopying or
other reprographic copying, a licence from Access Copyright (Canadian
Copyright Licensing Agency), 1 Yonge Street, Suite 1900, Toronto, ON M5E
1E5, fax (416) 868-1621.

Published by
Red Deer Press
A Fitzhenry & Whiteside Company
1512, 1800–4 Street S.W.
Calgary, Alberta, Canada T2S 2S5
www.reddeerpress.com

Credits
Edited for the Press by Peter Carver
Copyedited by Kirstin Morrell
Cover and text design by Erin Woodward
Cover illustration courtesy Jan Sovak
Cover images courtesy iStock and the Glenbow Museum
Printed and bound in Canada by Friesens for Red Deer Press

Acknowledgments
Financial support provided by the Canada Council, and the Government of
Canada through the Book Publishing Industry Development Program
(BPIDP).

THE CANADA COUNCIL | LE CONSEIL DES ARTS
FOR THE ARTS | DU CANADA
SINCE 1957 | DEPUIS 1957

National Library of Canada Cataloguing in Publication
Walsh, Alice, 1958–
A sky black with crows / Alice Walsh.
ISBN 0-88995-368-6
1. Title.
PS8595.A5847S58 2006   JC813'.54   C2006-905179-8

For D'Arcy

ACKNOWLEDGMENTS

$\mathcal{I}$ am grateful to Deannie Sullivan Fraser, Sharon Palermo, Welwyn Wilton Katz, Tyne Brown, Joan Clark and Barbara Little who have read the manuscript at various stages, offering valuable suggestions and feedback. My appreciation to Leona Trainer, my agent, for her support and encouragement. Many thanks, as well, to my editor, Peter Carver, for his invaluable comments and guidance along the way. Finally, I would like to extend my love and gratitude to my family, Dennis, D'Arcy and Christine Walsh.

The poem on page 16 is by Dillon Wallace, and is excerpted from his book *Grenfell of Labrador: a Story of his Life for Boys,* published by McClelland & Stewart in 1946.

Prologue

APRIL 1916

*I*t was a late spring afternoon, yet snow fell heavily upon the land. Ponds, lakes, and rivers were still frozen over and the ocean's heaving waves were trapped beneath the ice. Snug and warm inside the Carney Bay nursing station, Katie Andrews stretched lazily in front of the fire, listening to the logs crackle and fall. She enjoyed being inside, feeling the heat of the stove on her face. At times like this, it was easy to forget all the bad things that had happened. The pain she had felt for so long was little more than a dull ache.

Someone knocked at the door and, unwillingly, Katie pulled herself away from the chair and the comfort of the fire. She opened the door to a tall man who was so bundled up she could barely see his face. Snow glistened on the fur of his parka and ice clung to his eyebrows.

"Come on in," she said, opening the door wide.

The man stomped snow from his boots and removed his cap. "I'm Jimmy," he said, holding out his hand.

There was something familiar about the man's face. Katie tried to recall where she'd seen him before. She held out her own hand. "I'm Katie. How can I help you, sir?"

"A lot of sick people in Fox's Cove, Miss. We needs help."

Katie looked out the window at the swirling snow. Nurse Cameron was finally asleep after almost twenty-four hours. Katie herself had been awake since dawn.

Jimmy crossed the room to the woodstove, rubbing his hands together for warmth. "Such a long winter we're havin', Miss. Schooners will be some late comin' over from Newfoundland this year." He peered at her. "Didn't your family used to come down here on the boats?"

Katie stared again at the man's familiar face. "You're Etta's brother," she said, moving toward him. "Etta Duncan's brother?"

"Her cousin." He looked at her intently. "I remembers how you and Etta was such good friends. I remembers . . ."

PART 1

Chapter 1

THE VOYAGE—MAY 1913

*I*t was another late spring day, but nearly three years earlier, when Katie's family made their last trip to the Labrador. Katie remembered how crowded the government wharf was in Fathom Harbour that morning. Most of the people were freighters—families like Katie's, who didn't own a boat and had to be freighted down to the Labrador coast each season. They would be put off at places where they had left boats and houses the previous year.

The air was cool and scented with wood smoke. A slight breeze blew in off the ocean, bringing with it the taste of salt and melting ice. Gulls flew overhead, shrieking as they swooped down to grab the fish guts that had been thrown overboard from fishing boats.

Every year for as long as she could remember, Katie's family journeyed to the Labrador. And every year for as long as she could remember, the boats were always late. On this particular morning, they had waited nearly two hours before the vessel made her way into the harbor.

"About time!" someone shouted

"Looks like she's overcrowded already," someone else remarked. "Look how low she is."

Katie looked across the harbor at the approaching vessel and sighed knowingly. It was the same every season. In all the years she had been travelling to the Labrador, she couldn't remember a time when the boats had not been overcrowded. The small deck was always cluttered with crates, nets, salt, rope, oars, and casks of oil. Sometimes they were so overcrowded, there was barely standing room. And from the looks of things this trip was not going to be any different.

As the boat got closer, she could see the words *Mary March* stencilled in bold red letters on her side. People began pushing forward to the front of the wharf, some clinging to boxes and bundles. Many families brought furniture, boats, even goats, hens, and pets. Some of the animals were in cages, others tied to poles on the wharf.

Katie picked up her own belongings among the piles of bags, crates, and trunks that had accumulated on the wharf. She was grateful that her family only took what Mama called "the bare necessities." Their summer home had everything they needed, and they only brought clothing, bedding, and enough food to last them on the journey.

Katie looked wildly around for her family and spotted them among a crowd at the front of the wharf. Mama, she thought, looked pale and tired. She clutched a large iron pot while balancing Hannah on her hip. Papa was beside her, his arms loaded with blankets and baskets of food. Even Ruth, who was only six years old, struggled with a large jar of water.

"Two weeks of this," her father was grumbling when Katie met up with him on the ship's deck. "Longer, if we runs into bad weather or meets loose ice along the way."

The deck of the *Mary March* was already crammed, but still more people were crowding on, and more barrels, furniture, and animals were being loaded. Katie breathed in the faint odor of tar, fish, salt, and old net twine. She dropped her belongings on deck and, eyeing a wooden crate with a coil of rope on top, she let herself sink down beside it. She had been up since dawn, and it felt good to be off her feet. Leaning her head against the rope, she closed her eyes and listened to the bustle of activity, as fishermen and their families hurried up the gangplank and began moving about on deck. Just as she was starting to doze, something tugged at the sleeve of her sweater. Her eyes flew open, and she found herself face to face with a goat.

Katie sat up quickly. She could hear Ruth giggling nearby. A boy, not much older than herself, rushed toward her. Thick, black curls spilled out from under a knitted cap and his dark eyes were filled with concern.

"Joey," he scolded the goat, "I swears I'm gonna throw yeh overboard. He didn't hurt . . . " He stopped abruptly, staring at Katie. "Katie Andrews?"

"Matt?" Katie's mouth dropped open. She hadn't seen Matt Reid in over a year. Not since his father died and he moved away from Fathom Harbour to live with relatives.

"Nice to see you again, "Katie said. "Where do you live to now?"

"Heart's Desire," he told her.

Katie knew Heart's Desire was in Conception Bay. It wasn't far from St. John's, but a good two-hour boat ride from Fathom Harbour, which was in Trinity Bay. She tried to visualize the faded map of Newfoundland and Labrador that hung in the classroom behind Miss Carleton's desk. A long finger of land jutted out into the Atlantic, separating the two bays. Just a few days ago, the teacher showed them on the map the route they would be taking to Labrador. "You'll travel north from here," she had said, "all the way to Cape Bauld. From there, you'll cross the Belle Isle Strait and travel northward to Labrador."

"Come fall, Uncle Henry will be the new manager of the cooperative store in Red Bay." Matt explained. "His self and Aunt Mary will be moving to the Labrador."

"You'll be on the coast all winter?"

"Not me. I'm goin' to Bishop Field College in the fall. Uncle Henry thinks that all boys needs learning."

Katie had heard about Bishop Field College, a fancy boy's school in St. John's where rich merchants sent their sons. How could Matt's uncle afford such a place? She couldn't help feeling a pang of envy, knowing that *she* wouldn't be returning to school. Mama had not regained her strength since Hannah's birth, thirteen months ago, and Papa felt Kate was needed at home. "You already knows how to read and write and do sums," he had told her. "Besides, you're thirteen years old, a young woman."

Katie didn't bother to remind him that she was actually thirteen and a half. She knew that girls much younger than her had already left school to go into domestic service. But Katie had a dream. And now, just thinking of not being able to return to school was enough to bring tears of disappointment.

The boat's whistle gave a long, piercing shrill, jolting her back to the present.

"We're off," someone shouted, and Katie could feel the boat pulling away from the wharf.

"Lift me up." Ruth tugged at Katie's dress.

"Come here," Matt said. He lifted Ruth off her feet as easily as if she were a rag doll. Katie looked out over the crowd, at the widening space between the ship and the dock. White handkerchiefs fluttered up from the wharf as people shouted their good-byes. After a while, Fathom Harbour's twenty-six houses, fish stages, general store, church, and schoolhouse were losing dimension and becoming as indistinguishable as dabs of paint on an artist's pallet.

"Katie? Ruth?" Katie's mother appeared with a basket of food. "Come get somet'ing to eat."

"Mama, you remembers Matt Reid?" Katie paused as Matt took Ruth off his shoulder, and stood her on deck beside her mother. "He used to live up over the hill from us."

Mama pushed back a strand of graying hair from her thin, pale face. "Indeed I do. Nice to see yeh again, my son." She handed Hannah to Katie. "Would yeh like a bite to eat?"

"No, thanks," Matt said, after a moment's hesitation, "I better go make sure Joey's not botherin' nobody."

Katie watched him walk away, happy he was making the journey with them. Matt was different from most boys she knew. And he didn't shy away from her because she was a girl. She wondered what it was like to lose both parents at such a young age. Matt's mother died when he was still a baby. His father died from tuberculosis just a couple of years ago. Katie glanced at her own father and felt a rush of pity at the sight of his gnarled hands clutching a mug of tea. He rarely relaxed and his hands were always busy. When he was not out fishing, he busied himself mending nets or repairing lobster traps. She noticed he looked more tired than usual. There were dark bags around his eyes and his shoulder blades stuck out sharply under his flannel shirt. His clothes had been patched and repatched, and Katie knew they would give little protection from the cold, rough weather on the Labrador.

As she ate dried capelin and thick slices of homemade bread and molasses, Katie thought about the journey ahead of her. Because there was no place on the ship to cook meals, everything the family would eat for the next couple of weeks would be cold. If the weather held, everything would be fine. But bad weather sometimes meant having to take refuge in sheltered inlets.

"Must be as many as fifty of us crowded on this little twenty-five ton vessel," her father complained. "A disgrace 'tis."

"At least women and girls are allowed on deck," Katie said, trying to keep her voice light. "Some skippers would keep us below deck for fear we'd bring bad luck."

"No one 'ill keep *you* below deck, sparrow," Papa said softly.

Katie smiled. It had been years since her father called her sparrow, his pet name for her. He used to say she was like the Labrador Savannah sparrow, but he'd never say why.

"Is Papa not feelin' well?" she asked her mother after her father had gulped down his tea and moved away.

"He's right discouraged," her mother said grimly. "And no wonder. He's short on fishing gear this season and can't get no more credit." Her voice wobbled as she spoke. "This truck system is ruining us all. We goes to the Labrador every season and works like dogs to make the merchants rich."

Katie knew a little about how the truck system worked. She knew that all the fish her father caught belonged to the merchant. The merchants advanced credit on salt, twine, nets, clothing, and other supplies, then claimed the fishermen's catch at the end of the season. The most her father could expect after months of hard work was enough food to last through the winter months. Sometimes, at the end of a season, he was more in debt than when he started out.

The next day Katie told Matt about how discouraged her father had become. It was a gray day with a cold wind blowing in from the north. They were standing on deck looking out at the ocean. "It's not fair that the merchants should get so rich from our fish," she said.

Matt rested his hand heavily on her shoulder. "No, it's not fair," he said, gently. "But that's how it's always been. Maybe it's because nobody expects more."

The two lapsed into silence, lost in their own thoughts. The evening sun had gone away now, and a cold wind rippled the waves. It whipped Katie's long, red hair around her face and she could feel it cut through her knitted sweater like sharp needles. But only when large drops of rain plopped on the deck, did they scurry for shelter.

In the hours that followed, rain beat fiercely on the deck, and the sea turned a menacing gray. Katie and her family were herded below deck where hatches were closed tightly against the storm. She hated the dark, airless hold. Sometimes they could stay there for days without seeing the stars, the moon or the light of day. She held her hands over her ears to shut out the sound of moaning, crying babies, and the crashing of furniture and barrels on deck. Passengers threw up, sometimes missing the pails that were beside them. The air was stale with unwashed bodies and overflowing slop pails, and the stench became over-powering. Because the ship's hold was so close to the deck and beams, Katie had to be careful not to hit her head when she sat up.

Her stomach heaved as she fought waves of nausea. She was aware of her mother beside her, offering her sips of water. "Only little sips," she reminded gently whenever Katie tried to gulp the water. "Too much at once will only make you sicker."

After three days the wind subsided, the waves grew calmer, and Katie and her family went back up on deck again. It was such a contrast to the gloom below; she had to adjust her eyes to the daylight. The air felt fresher, and the endless miles of Atlantic Ocean looked calmer than it ever had. Icebergs glinted in the distance, and whales came up to the schooner, splash-ing and slapping at the water with enormous tails. Gracefully, they hurled themselves out of the water, then plunged beneath the surface again.

The weather held for the next few days, and Katie spent most of her time on deck. Thousands of seabirds swooped from rocks and cliffs, their cries filling the air like a chorus. She spotted dozens of other tall-masted ships sailing north, their decks crowded with freighters. Katie knew many of the boats were built and owned by their skipper. Most of them were about the size of the *Mary March* and were used mainly for fishing. Come winter, they would be hauled up on the dry dock until March when the sealing season began.

The ship stopped at coves and bays along the way, dropping off supplies. In some places more people got on. At night the ship rested in sheltered bays and inlets.

"We're makin' good time," her father commented, a week into the voyage. He pointed to some rounded hills in the distance. "That's Notre Dame Bay over there. We're already halfways there."

Then one morning, a little more than two weeks after they started out, the vessel moved slowly into a narrow tickle. Mountains, hills, and icebergs were reflected starkly in the calm water. Craggy cliffs towered around them, rising thousands of feet out of the sea. There were no trees, only rocks and barrens and a sky so blue it looked as if it had been painted.

Hannah came running toward Katie, holding a wooden doll their father had made her. The doll had painted on cheeks and eyes. Mama had made the doll's dress from a flour bag dyed with Partridge berries. "Kay-ee," she called.

Katie picked her sister up and hugged her close. She looked out at the lofty headlands and rounded, moss-covered hills. The boat was moving into Nellie's Tickle with its cluster of fishing huts and long wharves jutting out into the harbor.

Matt came to stand beside her. "This is where we get off," she told him.

"I'm going farther north, toward Indian Harbour," he told her.

"Will I see you again?" she asked.

"See again?" Hannah echoed, making them laugh.

"I'll be goin' to Fathom Harbour at the end of the season. I'd like to come and visit." He turned to Hannah. "Would yeh like that?"

"Like that," the baby repeated.

"I'd like that too," Katie said softly.

Chapter 2

THE LABRADOR

Katie awoke to the noisy fluttering and cawing of crows perched on the roof of their hut. Although a gray dawn still hovered outside the window, she knew Papa had left hours earlier to go fishing. Her mother and Ruth were still asleep in their wooden bunks, and she could hear Hannah snoring gently from the lobster crate that served as her cradle.

Slowly, Katie's eyes adjusted to the dimness. She could make out the shadowy shapes of a crude wooden table and chairs, a washstand in the corner, and a little iron stove with pipes that went through a hole cut in the roof. The walls were papered with pages from newspapers and magazines tinged brown and smelling of mold.

She groaned as she shifted her body. All her bones and muscles ached. Katie's first couple of days on the Labrador were spent helping her mother clean out ice and snow that had built up in the hut during the winter. They did this while her father helped put together platforms and fish flakes.

Katie sighed in the darkness. Her life would be different now that she wouldn't be going back to school. A wave of sadness washed over her as she thought about it. She had loved the one-room schoolhouse with the little potbellied stove. And since Miss Carleton came from Boston, school had become a real joy. The teacher owned a large collection of books that she let her students borrow. Stories by Charles Dickens and Jane Austen had kept Katie occupied for hours. Miss Carleton had even allowed her to bring a copy of *Oliver Twist* to the Labrador. The books opened up a whole new world to Katie, but there was another reason she wanted to go back to school. Reaching under her moss-filled mattress, she pulled out a photograph yellowed and cracked with age. In the semi-darkness, she could barely see the picture, but she had looked at it so often, the image was burned in her memory. It was a photograph of Great-aunt Til in her nurse's hat and uniform. Whenever Katie looked at it, she was filled with awe. She couldn't imagine anything more thrilling than to be able to wear a nurse's uniform. At the age of thirty-one, the year great Uncle Jack's boat went down, her aunt went into nursing. She even went to night school to learn how to read and write. Doctors had been concerned about nurses administering drugs when they couldn't read. Aunt Til was seventy-eight years old now, and had long given up nursing. She lived in a little house in Fathom Harbour, not far from where Katie lived. Katie knew she would always cherish the hours she spent in her kitchen listening to her stories. Her aunt helped with operations, administering anesthetic drop by drop on an open mask placed over the patient's nose and mouth. She had worked in the tuberculosis san and even in the Mental. But what Aunt Til enjoyed most was being an outport nurse, travelling by boat, by dog team, and even by foot to treat the sick.

Ever since she was a very little girl, Katie had wanted to be a nurse like Aunt Til. But these days girls needed at least a tenth grade education before they could go into training. Katie knew it was useless to tell her father about her dream. He would only accuse Aunt Til of filling her head with nonsense.

I *will* find a way to become a nurse, Katie promised herself as she put the picture back under the mattress and scrambled out of bed. She tugged a cotton dress over the petticoat her mother had made from a flour sack. She pulled on a pair of brown ribbed stockings, then her shoes. The water she poured from a pitcher into the enamel washbasin felt cold as she scrubbed her face and neck. She smoothed back wispy red tendrils of hair from her forehead. She tried to open the door quietly, but it squeaked loudly on its iron hinges. After a quick trip to the outhouse, she began her chores. She picked up a large butter tub that was used for carrying water from a nearby stream. Most mornings, Etta Duncan was waiting for her and they went to the stream together. Etta's family were <u>livyers</u> who moved to Nellie's Tickle each summer to fish.

permanut settler of Labrador

Katie walked slowly, savoring the crisp morning air that had just enough of a breeze to ruffle the dark blue water and keep away the black flies. She passed wooden and sod-covered huts, all with small square windows and crooked chimneys poking from their roofs. As she walked by the Duncans' sod hut, she half expected Etta to come running to greet her. But the latch on the door was drawn and no smoke rose from the chimney. Katie was grateful she didn't live in a sod hut like Etta's family. The inside was always gloomy, dank, and dark, and reminded her of a big, black hole.

At least the weather was good. Katie knew storms could come without warning, ripping fishing boats from their moorings and blowing chimneys and even roofs from buildings. But today, all was calm. Gigantic icebergs gleamed in the distance and patches of snow still lingered on the hills. Seagulls swooped and circled lazily, and to her delight, a Labrador Savannah sparrow was singing from a nearby bush. Papa often said that spring did not begin in Labrador until the Savannah sparrow had arrived.

She passed a cemetery with rows of tiny crosses. Her brother Luke was buried there. He had died before he reached his first birthday—before Katie was born. Their mother now referred to him as "poor little Luke," and she often reminded Katie that had he lived, he would be sixteen years old. "Almost a growed up man," she would say. "A hand for yer father in the fishin' boat."

Katie often felt a pang of sadness for her mother. She couldn't imagine what it would be like to lose Hannah or Ruth. Katie was seven when Ruth was born, and she remembered rocking her sister and singing to her, sometimes keeping her occupied for hours while their mother worked. But with Hannah it was different. Mama had been so ill after Hannah's birth that for months she was left completely in Katie's care. Katie always felt that Hannah was as much *her* baby as she was her mother's. She smiled now, thinking of her youngest sister. "The wild one," their father called her. Hannah could barely sit still for a moment. So different from Ruth who played quietly for hours.

Katie looked down the length of the deserted beach. Waves gently broke across the shore, receding back to the ocean. She found seashells, a piece of colored glass that had been washed ashore by the tides, and a coal-black feather that had been dropped by a raven in flight. As she walked, she chanted a poem her father had taught her. He had learned it from his own father, and it had been passed down from generation to generation:

> *When Joe Bett's p'int you is abrest,*
> *Dane's rock bears due west.*
> *West-nor' west you must steer*
> *'til Brimstone Head do appear.*
> *The tickle's narrow, not too wide,*
> *the deepest water's on the starboard side.*
> *When in the harbor you is shot,*
> *Four fathoms you has got.*

Papa often said that in a land like Labrador where there are no buoys, lighthouses or landmarks, poems like this one were the only way to guide the fishermen. "'Tis a dangerous coast with islands scattered every-wheres," he once said. "The man who sails it must know it like the back of his own two hands."

After reaching the stream, Katie knelt on a carpet of damp moss and, making a cup with her hand, drank thirstily. The water was the color of steeped tea, but it had a cool clean taste. After filling her tub, Katie headed back to the hut. The bucket was heavy, forcing her to walk slowly. Most of her neighbors were up by this time, and wisps of blue smoke rose gently into the still morning air. There were children in bare feet and women in faded brown and black clothing. They moved up and down the landwash, turning fish that had been spread on flakes to dry in the sun.

"Katie?" A tall girl with straight, black hair ran toward her.

Katie rushed forward and, in her eagerness, spilled some of the water. "Etta, I missed yeh this morning."

Etta smiled weakly, her face pale. "I got a real bad toothache," she said, rubbing her jaw with the back of her hand.

Before Katie could answer, she heard her mother calling. "Katie? Come get breakfast, so I can let the fire out. There's work to be done."

Katie touched her friend's shoulder. "Come by again when yeh feels better, Etta. I've got something I wants to show yeh."

Etta walked away, her hand still covering her face. Katie picked up the bucket of water and was heading toward the hut when she noticed a boat coming around the point. Tall white sails billowed like clouds in the mild breeze. Shading her eyes with her hands against the glare of the sun on the ocean, Katie watched as a lifeboat was lowered into the water. Two people—it looked like a man and a woman—began climbing down a rope ladder. By now, everyone had stopped working, and all eyes were on the boat as it rowed toward shore.

The man got out first, and held out his arm to the woman. He was wearing a waistcoat and top hat and he looked out of place on the landwash. The woman carried a parasol and wore an ankle-length skirt with a fancy blouse. After pulling the boat up on the beach, they approached the curious crowd, the woman stumbling on the sharp rocks in her fancy shoes. She was having difficulty holding up her dress and carrying the parasol at the same time. The man, who was rather plump, slipped once, and almost fell on the sharp beach rocks. He carried a small, brown, leather box under his arm, and as he got closer, Katie realized it was a camera.

"Good morning, folks," he said, as he approached them. "I'm Silas Abbot."

The women and children stared openly, but no one spoke. Katie wondered if Silas Abbott was a merchant.

"And this is my wife, Jane," he added.

Again, no one spoke.

Silas showed them his camera. "Would you mind if I took some photographs?"

"It's his hobby," Jane said, looking slightly amused as she glanced around at the women and children on the beach.

"A very serious hobby," Silas said. "Some of my work has been published by the National Geographic Society."

"Why would yous want to take snaps of we?" Maude Skinner dared to ask.

"I'm doing a series on the fisher folk."

"Oh, a series," Maude said, and Katie knew she hadn't the faintest idea of what the man was talking about.

"Is it okay then?" Silas asked, but he was already pointing his camera. "Pretend I am not here," he told them. "Just keep doing what you were doing before I arrived."

The women exchanged uneasy glances as they went back to work, and Katie knew they were uncomfortable having a stranger take pictures of them.

After a while, Hannah ran up to the woman and pressed a dried starfish in her hand. "For you."

Mrs. Abbott laughed. "What a beautiful little girl. So delightful to look at. Silas," she called, "take our picture."

As soon as the Abbotts returned to their boat, there was a buzz of conversation.

"What's they doin' here?"

"I wonders what they'll do with the snaps?"

"'magine, all dressed up like that on the landwash."

"S'pose they t'ought we was havin' a party."

Laughter.

⌁

A couple of days later when Katie and Etta went to the stream to get water, Katie carried a brown paper bag under her arm. After their buckets were filled, she opened it up. "I brought another book," she said, "*Oliver Twist*. It's by the same author who wrote *Great Expectations*. I'll read it to you as soon as I gets a chance."

Etta's eyes lit up. "Oh, Katie. I still got pictures in me head from that last book yeh read me. I can't understand how so many pictures can come about from just letters on a page."

Katie smiled, knowingly. "I brought yeh this too," she said, handing her friend a *Sears Roebuck* catalogue.

Etta's mouth dropped open. Books were almost unheard of on the Labrador, and she had never even seen a catalogue before. Sitting on a large rock, she eagerly flipped the pages, her eyes wide as she looked at the black and white drawings of rugs, jewellery, dolls, dishes, and furniture. She murmured little sounds of pleasure as she looked at mushroom-shaped hats decked with cherries, flowers, feathers, and ribbons. She lingered over nightgowns with delicate laced collars and sleeves. "So pretty," she commented.

"They're lovely," Katie agreed. "Expensive though." Prices ranged from forty-nine cents to one dollar and forty-eight cents.

She watched as Etta slowly turned the pages. When she came to a page of ladies' gowns, there was a sharp intake of breath. "Look at that," she said, pointing to a dress with elegant puffed sleeves. "I never seen nothing like that before." There was lace at the collar and down the front. The skirt had clusters of double tucks extending around to the back.

Katie looked at the price. "It costs twelve dollars and seventy-five cents."

Both girls lapsed into silence. Neither of them had ever seen that much money. In Labrador, everything was paid for in cod. Etta closed the book.

At that moment there was a shrill blast, and Katie saw smoke rising over the hills. Another boat was steaming into the harbor. She couldn't imagine who it might be. The *Kyle,* that delivered letters, parcels and supplies to all the little coves, bays, and tickles, had left a few days ago. She wouldn't be returning for weeks. No other boats were expected.

The girls hurried back to the beach. By this time everyone had stopped working and was standing at the water's edge. After a while, a large boat appeared around the point flying two huge flags. As she got closer, Katie could see the single word *Strathcona* on her side.

"It's Dr. Grenfell's hospital ship," she said, breathlessly.

Chapter 3

AUGUST 19-13

*B*y late evening, fish had been split and salted, the daily chores all finished. Fog had sneaked in along the coast, hanging heavily over the ocean and clinging stubbornly to the hills like damp cobwebs. Inside the cabin it was warm and cosy. Katie breathed in the pleasant fragrance of wood smoke mingled with the aroma of a beef stew that simmered in a big iron pot on the stove. Beside it, a pot of strong tea was brewing.

Papa was deep in conversation with Willie Blake who owned one of the nearby cabins. Willie's wife and baby had died a year ago, and he now came to the Labrador alone. Katie's family often invited him for supper.

Darkness came early, and Mama had already lit the kerosene lamp. As Katie put down plates and mugs on the plain wooden table, her thoughts were on Dr.

Grenfell. No sooner had the *Strathcona* dropped anchor than the fishing boats came back into the harbor. All day, boats filled with patients flocked to her deck for treatment. The ship had been so close to shore that Katie could make out the words, *God is Love,* on her main mast. How she would like to meet this man who had done so many strange and wonderful things. She had heard how the doctor once gave his clothes to a fisherman and swam back to the *Strathcona* in his underwear. Another time, he was traveling over the frozen sea with his dog team when the ice went adrift, cutting him off from shore. He had to spend the night on an ice pan and later wrote a book about his experience. Etta is the lucky one, Katie thought. She had actually gone aboard the boat and had a tooth pulled. When she came ashore, she told Katie about shelves filled with books, glass cases filled with pills and medicine. There were chairs covered with fancy embroidered cloth, and little brass pegs to hang coats and sweaters. "Bigger than any house I ever seen," Etta had declared.

"Supper's ready." Mama's voice broke into Katie's thoughts.

Everyone took a place at the table. Before they began eating, Katie's father bowed his head, thanking God for the many quintals of fish he had caught and asked for His blessing upon the family. Then Mama ladled the stew onto plates that she passed around the table.

Ruth held her hand over the kerosene lamp, making distorted shadows on the wall. Hannah laughed and clapped her hands.

"Ruthie, don't do that," Mama scolded. "You'll smoke the chimney all up."

Ruth sat back on her chair, disgruntled.

"I hopes little Annie will be okay," Mama said, sounding worried.

She was referring to Annie Lambert who they took away on the *Strathcona*. Annie was Ruth's age, a pale, sickly little girl who coughed all the time. When Annie's mother came ashore, she was crying. Mama had put her arm around her shoulder, her voice low and soothing.

"They'll take her across the strait to St. Anthony," Papa said. "They got a wonderful hospital over there with doctors and nurses. They'll make the youngster well again." He shook his head, his voice filled with awe. "Ninety-seven foot long, that hospital ship. One hundred and t'irty tons, a teakwood deck, iron hatches, and six hospital beds."

Willie nodded. "I seen the upper deck meself. There's a wheelhouse, a charthouse, and a steam winch."

"I remembers the first time the doctor came to the coast," Papa said. "It was in the *Albert.*"

Although Katie had heard the story many times, she listened with rapt attention. She had grown up with stories about how Dr. Grenfell had come from faraway England and built hospitals, cooperatives, and orphanages along the coast.

"When we got to the boat," her father continued, "Dr. Grenfell come out on the deck. 'I been sent here by the Mission to Deep Sea Fishers,' he tells us." He paused to put a dollop of molasses in his tea.

" 'Well my son,' says I, 'for sure, we needs a doctor around here.' " He looked around the table. "What, with as many as t'irty thousand fisherman and their families along the coast, and nobody around when they took sick."

"He operated on me own poor mother right on the kitchen table," Willie said, his voice filled with admiration. "I was just a lad then, no older than Ruthie here. But I remembers that the doctor saved a lot of lives that summer."

Mama piled more stew onto the big platter. "'Tis a pity he wasn't here when poor little Luke took sick with the fever," she said, in a quiet voice. "Or when dozens of other youngsters died from beri-beri, scurvy, TB, and the likes."

"Sometimes them things can't be helped," Willie said, quietly. "The good Lord chooses what's best for us." He lowered his dark eyes, and Katie wondered if he was thinking of his own wife and baby girl.

Everyone fell silent after that, and when Mama began clearing away the dishes, Katie got up to help, her thoughts still on Dr. Grenfell. She imagined him to be like the heroes in the books Miss Carleton had read to them in class. Katie knew the doctor had proposed to his wife before he even knew her name. Mrs. Grenfell never accompanied him on his voyages. The fact that no one had seen her made her seem more mysterious.

Long after supper was finished, Willie and Papa lingered at the kitchen table, drinking mugs of hot tea. Katie couldn't remember a time when she'd seen her father so at ease. "We got off to a good start," she heard him say. "Nearly fifty quintals of fish again today."

Dear Papa, Katie thought. He worked so hard for his family. Last season, all they gained was a few barrels of flour, some molasses, salt beef, butter, and tea. There was barely enough food to see them through the winter.

"If this keeps up," Papa continued, "we'll do all right this season. Perhaps the merchants might even let me have some of the gear I needs." His face looked hopeful in the soft light of the kerosene lamp.

"The merchant decides what price we pays for their goods," Willy said. "I don't think it's right for them to set the price for our fish too. It's what keeps us in debt to them."

"When Uncle Jack got drowned, his debt was passed on to his son, my cousin Eli," Papa continued. "Poor Eli spent most of his life paying it off. When he died it was passed on to his son." Papa shook his head. "Some of us are born in debt."

"But the day is comin' when we'll no longer be owned by the merchant." Willie said. "Dr. Grenfell already got a cooperative store going in Red Bay, and there'll be more. Someday we'll be free from this mercantile system, free from the debt that ties us to the merchants, makin' us slaves."

Chapter 4

SEPTEMBER 1913

*D*ark, gloomy rain clouds spread across the sky, and the cliffs cowered under the threat of a storm. The air was ominously still, and although there was not a ripple on its solemn gray surface, the sea seemed to be harboring old resentments. It was the kind of weather that made everyone listless. Animals nervously sniffed the air. Young children whimpered and whined. Even good-natured Hannah fussed and cried for no good reason. The older children wandered aimlessly about, getting in their mothers' way. Women found it difficult to get any housework done and spent most of the morning peering anxiously through their tiny windows. Years later, Katie would remember it as a day that set in motion a sequence of events that changed their lives forever.

Around mid-morning, she and Etta went to the mesh to pick bakeapples. The berries were so ripe they fell off the leaves, squishing between their fingers. A cloud of blackflies circled their heads, so thick the air around them looked black. They crawled down Katie's neck, in her ears, and up her nose.

"It's hard to believe the fishing season is almost over," Etta said. She gazed toward the ocean where the fog had moved in like a heavy curtain. It blotted out the sky and the jagged cliffs.

"We still have a few more weeks left."

"Seems like we hardly had no time together."

Katie realized this was true. They had been kept busy nearly every minute taking care of younger children, spreading fish, and helping with the housework and other chores. "There's always next season," she reminded her friend.

"I don't know," Etta said sadly. "I'll be going into service soon. Papa's been asking around for a job for me. I may go to the mainland, maybe even to Canada."

"Will yeh miss your family?" Katie asked.

"Of course I'll miss them. But there's not a lot for a girl to do on the Labrador in winter."

"Things are going to be different for me, too," Katie said, her voice sad. "I won't be goin' back to school. Papa says I'm needed at home. He feels that since I knows how to read and write, there's no need to go back." Katie picked at the hem on her dress. "I will go back someday, though. I wants to be a nurse."

"A nurse?" Etta's dark eyes were filled with awe. "I never met anyone who wanted to be a nurse before. You're so lucky to have gone to school, Katie. I wish I could learn to read and write." She tucked her legs under her cotton dress to keep them warm. "Papa says that if I gets into service in St. John's or some other big city, I might be able to go to night school. I'd love to be able to read from books."

Katie couldn't imagine never having gone to school, or not being able to read or write. It must be rough living on the coast year round.

"What's it like out there, Katie?"

She knew Etta meant the world beyond Labrador. She didn't quite know how to answer her friend, having never strayed far from Fathom Harbour herself. Katie told her about a cousin who went to St. John's and got a job in Smallwoods' boot factory. He wrote home telling about the many shops and restaurants, tall buildings, and large stone churches. She told Etta about the merchants' wives. Papa once said they spent their time driving around in fancy carriages, dressed in silk and lace and acting like queens.

The girls lingered on the mesh, more interested in talking than in picking berries.

Then, without warning, there was a fluttering of wings overhead, and the sky turned black.

"Crows," Etta said. "Must be a big storm on the way."

There were thousands. The air was alive with their woeful cries. They had come inland from the water seeking shelter behind rocks and in the crevices of the cliffs. No sooner had they arrived than a sudden wind came up. The ocean rose and swelled in black swooping waves. Dark clouds loomed above them. Drops of rain splattered Katie's bare legs, making her shiver. "C'mon," she told Etta. "We better get the fish in before it all spoils." She glanced anxiously toward the ocean, knowing that her father, along with other men and boys, were still out there.

By the time they got back to their huts, rain was pelting down. Women and children moved quickly, grabbing fish from flakes and rocks. Long before the last fish was stored away, the girls were soaked, their hair plastered against their heads. Katie felt chilled to the bone.

From where they stood, they could see the tiny boats struggling to get back to land. Waves broke in a fury against the rocks. Only a few fishermen had made it safely to shore. Katie said a prayer for the safe return of her own father and for those who were still out on the tossing waves.

By late afternoon, most of the fishermen had come back. Boats were hauled up on the landwash. Doors were closed tightly against the storm, and children and animals were called inside. There was still no sign of Katie's father.

"It's gettin' worse out," Katie said, her voice filled with fear. Waves broke in a fury against the rocks. Rain lashed against the roof of the hut, and the small square of glass in the window rattled ominously. Lightning shot across the sky, and thunder crashed and rumbled.

"Your father's a good seaman," Katie's mother tried to reassure her. "Don't yous go worrying about nothin'. I knows he'll be here by and by."

The hours ticked slowly by. Darkness was falling and still Papa had not returned.

"Set the table, Katie," her mother said. "We'll go ahead and eat. I'll keep yer father's supper warm on the back of the stove. By the time he gets ashore, he'll be half-starved."

Katie put down five tin plates and five mugs. Beside it, she placed as many forks, knives, and spoons. Just seeing her father's place set for him made her feel better.

Mama ladled up generous helpings of partridge stew and dumplings. Katie picked at her food, conscious of her father's empty chair at the head of the table. A queasiness rolled in her stomach, making it hard to swallow.

Her mother kept up a steady flow of conversation. "Your father is right pleased with all the fish he caught. When we gets back to Newfoundland, you and Ruth will need new coats for winter."

"Can yeh buy me a red coat, Mama?" Ruth's blue eyes were eager as she looked up from her plate of stew. Two small braids fell against her pale face. Katie realized she was too young to know the danger their father was in.

A faint smile touched Mama's lips. "We'll get yeh a red coat, Ruthie," she promised.

"With white fur on the collar, Mama? Like the one I seen in the Sears Roebuck catalogue."

"My, we're some fancy this evening," Mama teased. "If I didn't know better, I'd think yeh was the daughter of some St. John's merchant." But then she added softly, "We'll get Ruthie a red coat with white fur on the collar. And yer father . . ." her voice caught, "yer father needs new trousers."

Outside, the wind blew in fierce gusts, and the sea thundered against the cliffs. Enormous waves came almost up to the cabin door.

Long after Katie and Ruth were in bed, Mama lingered by the window where she had placed a candle. She was darning socks, but Katie often caught her glancing through the small square of glass.

Katie lay awake for a long time, tossing in her bed. All the stories she had heard about fishermen lost at sea came back to her. Boats were lost every year on the Labrador. The razor-edged rocks were sharp enough to cut a small boat in half. Icebergs floated freely, and could crush a boat as quickly as a boot could crush a moth. During one storm, eighty vessels were lost. Seventy men lost their lives, and two thousand men, women, and children were stranded on the coast.

After a troubled two-hour sleep, she awoke at dawn to find that the wind had dropped. Hannah was awake in her makeshift crib. Katie picked her up, snuggling the baby's warm body against her own. Mama was fully dressed and standing by the window. From the dark shadows that rimmed her eyes, Katie knew she had not slept the whole night.

She went to the window and glanced out. All was calm now. The landwash was littered with bits and pieces of wood, broken oars, nets, traps and pieces of rope. A lone black boot rested near the edge of the ocean.

Katie tightened her hold on the baby.

"I knows he'll come back to us," Mama said, her voice sounding hollow in the quiet of the cabin. She twisted her wedding ring on her finger. "Somebody, somewheres *must* have picked him up."

Chapter 5

OCTOBER 1913

*K*atie waited anxiously as days and weeks dragged by. The fishing season drew to a close, and the fishing stages were taken down for another season. The mail boat dropped off the last of the winter supplies, her whistle sounding long and lonely as she pulled away. Vessels began making their way back to Newfoundland, but there was still no news about her father.

When Katie was little, she remembered asking her father after a long season on the Labrador when they would be going home again. He would always tell her that when the Savannah sparrow took flight, they too would leave. The Savannah sparrow had long gone now, but Katie's mother refused to go home. Twice, she told them the story of how Uncle Jim had been lost at sea. "The whole family was all packed, ready to go back to Newfoundland when back he comes. I expects yeh father to do the same."

As much as Katie wanted to believe this, she was filled with troubling doubts.

Etta came to say good-bye. Her family was moving back to their winter home in a sheltered inlet. "I hopes yeh father gets back before the ocean freezes," she said, a note of worry creeping into her voice.

Katie hugged her friend, blinking back tears. Willie Blake tried to persuade Katie's mother to go home. He had stopped by their cabin a number of times since Papa went missing, and the day before he went back to Newfoundland he came again. "Come winter, you'll all freeze to death," he reasoned, looking around the small cabin. "My dear woman, you got to get yerself and the young ones away from here."

"We're not going nowheres," Mama said firmly. "John'll be back, and I wants to be here when he does."

Willie shook his head sadly, his narrow face filled with concern. "When the ocean freezes over, yous'll be beyond reach 'til late spring. And if them easterly winds pushes the arctic ice against the coast, it could hold it there 'til June."

"John'll be back," her mother said, unyielding.

"Well, if yeh changes your mind . . ."

Willie left them wood and some tea and molasses. "Take care now," he said, patting Katie's arm before letting himself out.

Katie knew they should leave the Labrador. Never before had she doubted her mother's decisions, but during the last few weeks, Mama had turned into a stranger. Her eyes had a sad, haunted look, and her face sagged with tiredness. Day after day she sat by the window, staring out at the ocean, paying little attention to Katie and the younger girls. She had begun to cough more and more, a deep, hacking cough that racked her thin body. Katie's parents had always taken good care of them, always made things right. But now Papa was dead and Mama had become silent and withdrawn. Katie knew it was up to her to take care of the family. She made sure that Ruth and Hannah ate properly and were dressed warm. She urged her mother to eat so that she could keep up her strength.

The days grew shorter and the nights were so cold Katie didn't bother to get undressed. When she awoke each morning, the air was colder than the morning before. Ducks and geese passed overhead and the green moss on the hills turned yellow. Most mornings the ground was covered with a hard frost. She picked blueberries and bakeapples from the marsh, and looked for driftwood along the shore. The huts were all boarded up for winter, giving them a haunted look.

The stillness of everything gave Katie an uneasy feeling. She felt a tight knot of nervousness in her stomach. She worried about her family, worried how Mama would get them back to Newfoundland. Even if Papa did return, how would they get home in his small boat?

One morning she awoke to find that the water in the washbasin had frozen during the night.

All the signs were there and she couldn't ignore them: winter was coming. Willie Blake's words came back to her. *You'll be out of reach 'til late spring.*

There was not enough food to see them through the winter months, and their clothes were not warm enough for the harsh Labrador winter. Katie tried to fight the panic that rose within her. There wouldn't be neighbors around to help, and they'd be all alone to face brutal blizzards.

Ruth complained of a sore throat. "It feels right scratchy, and it hurts," she said. The next morning she was burning up with a fever.

Then Mama got sick. Beads of sweat gathered on her forehead and upper lip, and her thin body was seized by spasms of coughing. Katie realized with great alarm that she was alone on the Labrador coast with two sick people. She kept a close watch on Hannah, keeping her as warm as she could. She knew that any sickness would be harder on a small child. She shuddered, remembering the many tiny markers in the cemetery. Katie brought Ruth and Mama cups of milkless tea, and tried to make them as comfortable as she could. She kept the fire going night and day and worried about the dwindling pile of wood.

During this time, something inside Katie had changed. She somehow felt older than her thirteen years. She was totally responsible for her sisters now, and with the weight of that responsibility came a chill of loneliness. Days passed. Katie lost all track of time. Her birthday was October 26, and she didn't know if that date had already gone by. Neither Ruth nor Mama seemed to be getting better. Her mother still coughed a lot, and she cried out in her sleep. One morning, while Katie was trying to get her to drink, she opened her eyes and looked up at her. Her lips moved and Katie saw she was trying to speak.

"What is it, Mama?"

Her voice was so low, Katie had to strain to hear. "Take care of your sisters, Katie."

"Of course, Mama, and I'll take good care of you too."

"Promise . . . Katie. Take good care of them."

Katie reached down and held her mother's hand. It

was cold and clammy. "They'll be fine, Mama," she tried to reassure her. "I'll take good care of them."

Wearily, her mother closed her eyes, and Katie tucked the blanket around her. She stayed with her until she drifted off to sleep.

Katie became exhausted—drained of all energy. Her head buzzed and her throat hurt when she swallowed. She was making Ruth a cup of tea when dizziness enveloped her. The room swayed and she barely made it to the narrow bunk. Hours later, she too was burning up with a fever.

Between bouts of delirium, Katie remembered her promise to take care of her sisters. Sometimes she'd open her eyes to see Hannah standing near the bed, her wooden doll clutched to her chest. Katie struggled to keep her eyes open. Weariness weighed her down like beach rocks.

She lost track of all time, and after what might have been hours or days later, she awoke to the sound of people talking and moving about. Voices, low and urgent, filled the cabin. Snatches of conversation reached her ears, and she wondered if she was dreaming. Too tired to sit up, she closed her eyes against the jumble of voices and drifted into an exhausted sleep.

Chapter 6

ST. ANTHONYS HOSPITAL

*B*etween sleep and wakefulness, Katie sometimes caught fragments of conversation. The voices were English, but different from her own. They sounded like the traveling dentist who came to Fathom Harbour once every two years. She remembered how they used to laugh at the funny way he pronounced his words. Their teacher firmly reminded them that the poor man came from England. He couldn't help the queer way he talked. Once she opened her eyes to see a woman in a nurse's uniform sitting beside her, but Katie was so tired, she closed her eyes and drifted back to sleep.

When she awoke again, the nurse was still beside her. She was young and had a full round face. Her blonde hair was short beneath her nurse's cap. A badge pinned to her lapel announced that she was

Gwen. Katie struggled to sit up. In a bed across from her, a woman was knitting a pair of socks. Her eyes rested on Katie. "The poor girl just woke up," she informed the nurse.

"What is this place?" Katie asked, lifting her head from the pillow.

The nurse smiled, although her eyes were sad. "It's a hospital," she said. "St. Anthony's hospital."

Katie stared at her, confused.

Gwen fixed a curtain around the hospital bed, shielding Katie from prying eyes. "You were brought here on the *Strathcona.*"

"Dr. Grenfell's hospital ship?"

The nurse nodded, dolefully. She explained that Willie Blake had been concerned. He had asked Dr. Grenfell and his crew to look in on Katie's family during the *Strathcona's* last visit to Labrador. "By the time they got there, you were all very sick," she said. "The cabin was freezing cold."

"What about my mother? And . . . Ruth and . . . ?"

Katie saw a shadow pass over the nurse's face. She covered Katie's hand with her own. "Your little sister is doing just fine," she said. "But your mother, Katie . . ." She swallowed as if she was having difficulty getting out the words. "Your mother . . . didn't make it. I am so sorry, my dear."

The words whirled frantically around in Katie's mind. For a few seconds, nothing registered as her mind struggled to grasp their meaning.

"Your mother had been sick for a long time," the nurse said gently. "She had tuberculosis. And when Dr. Grenfell found her, she had pneumonia on top of that." A note of sadness crept into her voice, "There was nothing anyone could do."

The hospital room seemed to waver around Katie. She heard a strangled gasp and realized it was her own. The nurse's arms came protectively around her. "Cry, if you must," she said kindly.

But Katie didn't cry. Her grief was too great for tears. Later, she would feel the sharp pain of loneliness, a loneliness that filled the hollow places inside her. Even now, years later, the memory brought a hurtful tightness to her chest. Like a dark shadow in a lighted room, the pain was always with her. First her father, now her mother. She had lost them both. She buried her face in her pillow, remembering Mama's last words: *Take care of Ruth and Hannah, Katie.* Did her mother know then that she wouldn't make it? She burrowed beneath the covers, and after a while, she fell into a fitful sleep, shivering against the starched hospital sheets.

During the next couple of days, she slept often, drifting in and out of dreams. She'd awake to find

Gwen sitting by her bed. "Your little sister will be by today," she told Katie one afternoon.

"Ruth?" Katie felt a pang of sadness. Ruth and Hannah were her only family now. She thought of Ruth's quiet, shy ways. And Hannah. Dear little Hannah who loved and trusted everyone. Katie was responsible for them now. She vowed she would do everything she could to make their life easy. All they had were each other.

"What about Hannah?" Katie asked. "Will I be able to see Hannah too?"

"Hannah?"

"My youngest sister."

Gwen peered at her closely. "I don't understand," she said. "I was sure Dr. Grenfell said there were just the two of you. He's in Canada now. It will be weeks before he returns."

"Hannah's the baby," Katie told her. "She's eighteen months old." A wave of alarm washed over her. "She's got to be here!"

Gwen got up, looked around the ward, and gestured to a tall nurse. They talked in low murmurs. Katie listened to snatches of their conversation. "Says . . . a younger sister . . . don't know . . . only Ruth . . ." As they talked, Katie fought to control the panic that was building inside her. She remembered how

Hannah would run and hide whenever strangers came. It had become a game with her. *Oh, dear God. What will happen to her if she's been left alone on the Labrador?* Images, too horrible for words, slithered into Katie's mind.

The nurse left the ward and Gwen returned to sit with Katie. "I've sent Nurse Allen to check," she said. Katie could not help noticing her worried look.

After what seemed like a long time, Nurse Allen returned, followed by an older nurse with graying hair. Katie studied her face, but it communicated nothing. She beckoned to Gwen, and once again there was murmured conversation. Katie couldn't hear what they were saying, but she could see the nurse was frowning. Gwen's face took on a crumpled look, and in that instant Katie knew Hannah was missing. No longer able to fight the waves of panic that engulfed her, she leapt up from the hospital bed. "No." She shouted frantically. "I have to find my sister. I have to go back to Labrador." All three nurses rushed to her side. A wave of dizziness overtook her and Gwen caught her before she blacked out.

When Katie opened her eyes again, she was confused. Then everything came back to her in a rush. "Hannah," she kept repeating. "I've lost Hannah."

"I'll call Mr. Payne," said one of the nurses. "He has a wireless. He'll get in touch with the Hudson Bay Company. They'll look for your sister."

Gwen tried to comfort her, but it was no use. Katie buried her face in the pillow. How could she have so carelessly lost Hannah? And she had promised Mama—promised her on her deathbed that she would take care of her sisters. Her mother had counted on her, and Katie had let her down. A desperate aching filled her chest. She felt completely alone. She closed her eyes, willing blackness to swallow her up.

For weeks she had trouble sleeping. She awoke in the middle of the night, gripped by a horrible sense of anxiety. She thought of the last time she'd seen Hannah standing in the cabin, her doll hugged close to her chest. Katie cried softly in the darkness, unable to get back to sleep.

In time, she got used to the routine of the hospital. She got used to being awakened early each morning, got used to the smell of antiseptics and the glare of electric lights. It was the first time she'd seen electric lights, and it was magical the way they switched on and off. The hospital workers brought her soup, porridge, stews, and other good food on trays, but she was never hungry. Her thoughts were always on Hannah, her grief so great she was inconsolable. Relatives and friends in Fathom Harbour had been contacted, but with the mail being so slow at this time of the year, Katie didn't know if they had received the news. Ruth was brought to see her. Her thin brown hair was woven into two stiff little braids, making her face look thin and pinched. Katie's heart wrenched at the sight of her. She wondered who had told her about their mother and Hannah, and how she received the news. Katie knew she had to get well for both Hannah and Ruth's sake. She would go look for Hannah as soon as the ice left the straits.

Gwen was what Aunt Til would have called a comforting spirit. She visited Katie nearly every day, offering kind and soothing words. There was something about her manner that Katie found reassuring. "It's a terrible thing to lose a sister," Gwen once said, talking as much to herself as to Katie.

"Why did you decide to become a nurse?" Katie asked her, one day.

"Stories of Florence Nightingale." She laughed. "I guess I had a romantic notion of what it was all about. But I soon learned that nursing is a trying, often difficult profession." She paused. "One that is very satisfying, of course." She looked at Katie. "Let me guess. You are thinking about becoming a nurse?"

"Yes," Katie admitted. "For as long as I can remember."

"Then you should." Gwen said. "I know it won't be easy, Katie. But if you want to be a nurse, you should make it your goal."

Physically, Katie grew stronger, and after a couple of weeks was able to get out of bed. But inside, she felt as if she had died. Where her heart should have been, there was only a cold, aching lump. Although she couldn't shed any tears, at night her mind cried out for all that she had lost.

After a while, Ruth was brought to see her every day and became Katie's only source of comfort. She thanked God she still had Ruth.

She spent many hours gazing numbly out the window. Low hills rose in the distance, and small rectangle shaped houses dotted both sides of the harbor. Near the hospital were a number of buildings that belonged to the mission, some with scripture verses written on them in large black letters: *FAITH, HOPE, AND LOVE ABIDE; BUT THE GREATEST OF THESE IS LOVE*. At the edge of the harbor was a large wooden building with the words, *SUFFER THE LITTLE CHILDREN* written over the door. There were rope swings out front, and children played in the yard. Katie thought the building was a school until she noticed that the children went inside during the evening. There were two children, a girl and a boy, both about Hannah's age. Katie remembered pushing Hannah on a swing in their back yard, a memory that twisted her heart.

"What is that building down there?" Katie asked Gwen one morning.

"That's an orphanage. Dr. Grenfell started it a number of years ago, and now they have dozens of children."

"An orphanage!" Katie immediately thought of Oliver Twist, and the orphanage where he spent his early years. She shivered, remembering greedy Mrs. Corney who starved the orphans, pocketing most of the money allotted for their keep.

Two weeks went by before Katie found out what happened to Hannah. The head nurse delivered the news, a large woman who looked quite pleased with herself. "The baby is in good hands," she informed Katie. She went on to tell her how a crew member on the hospital ship found a family who wanted to adopt Hannah. At first, Katie felt only relief. The hard knot of anxiety she carried in her stomach started to dissolve.

"She's a lucky little girl," the nurse continued. "She's found a family who cares for her."

Katie felt a prickle of resentment. Hannah already had a family who cared for her. Katie and Ruth were her real family. Didn't Papa always say that families belonged together? Since her parents' death, the bond she shared with her sisters somehow felt stronger. Hannah belonged to them, and Katie vowed she would get her back again.

One morning while she was staring out the window, a man walked into her room. He had a mustache neatly curled at both ends, and his gray-blue eyes crinkled at the corners. "You must be Kate," he said. "I'm Dr. Grenfell. It was my hospital ship that rescued you."

Katie could feel her heart pounding. She had always wanted to meet Dr. Grenfell, and now he was standing in front of her. And he had called her Kate. The name seemed more grown-up than Katie. She was surprised to see that the doctor was so ordinary looking. Not quite as large as she expected. His gray hair stuck straight up, and there were holes in the sleeves of his knitted sweater.

"Well, Miss," he said calmly. "Can't keep you in the hospital anymore. Hospitals are for sick people. It's time we sent you home."

Home? But where would she go? Katie slumped against the window. "We don't have a home," she said, finding her voice.

"Have you any relatives at all? An aunt? A grandmother?"

Katie shook her head. "There's only Aunt Til. She's

all crippled up with arthritis. Besides, she lives in Trinity Bay."

The doctor nodded. There was no need putting into words what they both knew. Katie was hundreds of miles from home. She might as well be in China. Besides, it would be better to stay in St. Anthony if she was going to return to Labrador in the spring.

A smile touched the doctor's lips, as he came to stand beside Katie at the window. He pointed to the large building down by the water. "That's my orphanage," he said. "It got started seven years ago with seven children. Miss Eleanor Storr came from England and is doing a fine job running the place."

Katie's mouth fell open. Surely he didn't expect her to take Ruth to live in an orphanage.

"Is there a job I can do at the hospital?" she asked. She thought of the girls—aides they called them— who brought around the food trays and made the hospital beds. Katie could do this kind of work. "I'm really a good worker," she added. "And I'll do anything."

The doctor shook his head, his eyes sweeping over Katie's thin frame. "You have been through a very serious illness," he said. "You will need to rest for several months. We don't want you to have a relapse."

Chapter 7

NOVEMBER 1913

"It'll be just 'til the ice leaves the harbor," Katie whispered to Ruth as they walked through the door of Dr. Grenfell's orphanage. Katie carried a small bag that held all their belongings. She squeezed her younger sister's hand. "I'll take good care of you," she promised.

A slim woman in a plain cotton dress greeted them. "I'm Eleanor Storr," she said. "Welcome, Katie and Ruth." Her dark hair was twisted in a loose knot at the back of her head, and her eyes looked friendly behind her round glasses.

Katie looked around her, taking in her surroundings. The room was large with windows that looked out over the ocean. Most of the furniture looked old and shabby, and the walls were covered in brown burlap.

"This is Katie and Ruth," Miss Storr told the children, who were quietly sizing up the new orphans.

There were six of them in the room, including a baby who sat on the lap of a girl who looked to be about Katie's age. Two little boys were sitting by a bookcase near the window. One of the children—a little girl on crutches—gave Katie a wide smile. She was short and stout with a flat face and black hair. Katie had seen children like her on the Labrador, and knew she was an Eskimo.

Katie swallowed hard. She couldn't believe she and Ruth were going to live here. She gave her sister's hand another squeeze, more to reassure herself than Ruth.

Miss Storr introduced the other children. "This is Emily," she said, gesturing toward the girl holding the baby. *Emily*. A pretty name for a pretty girl, Katie thought. Emily's skin was white and delicate, her cheeks rosy. Two yellow braids were twisted and pinned at the back of her head.

"The baby is Amy," Miss Storr continued, and as if on cue the baby gurgled, kicking her feet wildly. "And this is Kirkina," she said of the little girl with the crutches. "And this one," she said, touching the smallest child on the head, "is Martha." The little girl broke into wild giggles. She was about five years old with brown ringlets and dark eyes.

Miss Storr pointed across the room. "And over there, hiding behind the bookcase, is Ben." A boy of about eight with red hair and freckles peeped out at her. He smiled, and Katie saw that his front teeth were missing. "Next to Ben is Joseph." A blond boy eyed her warily from across the room.

The children didn't appear to be starving or neglected, Katie thought. They were all wearing clean clothes and looked happy. And Miss Storr seemed nice. Maybe it wouldn't be too bad living here after all.

More children came from downstairs and from outside, and Miss Storr introduced them all. Tommy, Mary, Ellen, Leah, and Jimmy. Katie couldn't imagine what it would be like living with so many people. She looked for the two toddlers she had watched from the hospital window, but they were nowhere around.

"Where's them girls from the Labrador to?" A woman appeared in the doorway. She was rather small with a wild mop of gray hair that stuck out in all directions. Her arms were as thin as mop sticks, and her shoulder blades stuck out sharply under her faded cotton dress. Her movements were quick and her small, black eyes darted around the room.

"Who's you?" she demanded, walking up to Ruth. The little girl's mouth dropped open, and she moved closer to her sister. She stared at the woman with large, frightened eyes. Even Katie drew back a little.

"Whas wrong? Cat got yeh tongue?"

Miss Storr put a protective arm around Ruth. "That's Birdie, our housekeeper," she said, calmly. "She is really a nice lady, and the best cook in the world. Birdie, this is Katie and Ruth, the two girls I have been telling you about."

Birdie's black eyes took in every inch of them. Then, with small crooked fingers she felt the material of Ruth's jacket. "Humph," she said, scornfully, "that's not fit for the cold weather. If you bees good, I might make yeh a decent coat." She peered into Ruth's face. "You're good, I hope." Then without another word, Birdie walked out of the room while Katie stared after her.

"Emily," Miss Storr spoke to the girl with the braid. "Katie will be sharing your room. Could you please show her where it is while I get little Ruth settled?"

Katie swallowed her disappointment. She had been hoping to share a room with her sister.

Without a word, Emily handed the baby to Miss Storr. She led Katie up a flight of rickety stairs to a room at far end of a narrow hallway. The ceiling was slanted, and the brown wooden floor had a bright homemade rug in the centre. There were two narrow iron beds covered with patchwork quilts and a small chest of drawers.

There was hardly enough space to walk around the two beds. "At least we got a room to ourselves,"

Emily said. "The other rooms got as many as six to eight beds."

Katie nodded. She was used to having very little space, and the room with its homemade quilts and colorful rugs looked cosy and pleasant.

"I hopes you'll like it here," Emily said shyly. "I likes it, but sometimes I misses Ma and Pa."

Katie thought of her own parents, a sense of loss surging through her.

"I won't get to see them 'til June," Emily added. "That's when school gets finished here."

Katie stared at her, surprised. "They're not dead?"

"Oh, no," Emily told her. "They lives on the Labrador. They sent me here so that I might get some learning."

"But I thought all the children here was orphans."

"Ben and Joseph is orphans," Emily said. "And so's Martha and some of the others. Kirkina's parents lives on the Labrador. I heard Miss Storr say that a lame child is useless on the Labrador where people got to travel for food. I guess that's why Kirkina was sent here. They're others like me who was sent here to get learning."

"Are there many babies?" Katie asked, remembering the two little ones she used to watch from the hospital window.

"There's just Amy now," Emily said. "And she'll be leaving soon. Dr. Grenfell found a home for her in Canada. He don't think an orphanage is a good place to raise babies. He tries to find homes for them in Canada and the States."

Emily went downstairs, leaving Katie alone in the room. This would be her home until at least spring. How could she get used to living with so many people? She tried to comfort herself with the fact that she would be able to go to school again, but all she could feel was emptiness . . . loneliness. Her world had fallen apart, and she felt nothing could make it right again.

Chapter 8

DECEMBER 19-13

"Are you settling in well?" Gwen asked one day while Katie was visiting her at the hospital.

"The children's home is not what I expected," she admitted. She laughed. "I guess I've been reading too much of Dickens."

Gwen was thoughtful. "Charles Dickens used fictional characters, but he was writing about real conditions in England at the time. My grandfather actually met Mr. Dickens. Met him shortly after he published his first novel." She smiled at Katie. "Anyway, I am glad you are doing well."

Katie nodded. She didn't tell her friend how she often woke in the middle of the night thinking she was in her own bed in Fathom Harbour. Like a heartless intruder, memories of the past weeks would rush back to her. At times, the pain of her loss was almost unbearable.

"I have something to tell you," Gwen said, looking at Katie. "Some weeks ago, I applied for a position at the Victoria General Hospital in Halifax. I got word yesterday that there's a job opening. I will be leaving in a couple of weeks."

She sucked in her breath. "I'll miss you, Gwen."

Gwen smiled at her. "I'll miss you too, of course. But I will write often—I promise."

Katie walked home from the hospital with an empty, aching hollow beneath her ribs. Gwen's friendship was important to her. Since her parents' death, she sometimes experienced loneliness like nothing she'd felt before. Often she lay awake at night thinking about them. She was only ten when Papa taught her to steer a komatic hauled by a dog team. First, she practised running the dogs across the frozen sea before taking them along a narrow path through the woods. Papa used to brag that she could handle a komatic as well as any adult. Katie often thought of Aunt Til too. She had been contacted, of course. She sent a telegram, asking if Katie and Ruth would be returning to Fathom Harbour in the spring. Katie knew she couldn't leave until she found Hannah.

There was plenty to do at the children's home. She had school and lessons. She swept and scrubbed floors, sorted and washed laundry. Even Ruth and the younger children had chores to do, and were kept busy dusting and polishing, and helping with the dishes and laundry. Miss Storr taught all the girls cooking, rug hooking, sewing, and home nursing. The orphanage had a small library with comfortable chairs and a good selection of books. Katie made friends with the children, and Birdie and Miss Storr were kind to her.

It pleased Katie that Ruth was adjusting so well. There was color in her cheeks, and she laughed and played with the other children. She and Kirkina became quick friends, and Katie would often see the two little girls whispering on the stairs or giggling at the supper table.

Katie comforted herself with the thought that as soon as the strait was free from ice, she would return to Labrador to search for Hannah. A new hospital, *The Emily Chamberlain,* had opened at North West River, and Birdie told her they were looking for strong young girls to make beds, do laundry, and cook meals for the patients. After she had Hannah with her, she would save enough money to finish her education so that she could go into nursing.

The temperature dropped lower and lower each night, and a raw wind blew in off the Atlantic. Frost hardened the ground, and sometimes a thin, lacy pattern of snow dusted the windows and roofs of the mission buildings. Early in December, Katie awoke to the first real snowfall of the season. The snow was already a foot deep, and flakes as large as goose feathers were still falling steadily.

The younger children had been talking about Christmas and Sandy Claws for weeks, and this first snowfall heightened their excitement. Katie helped them write letters to Sandy Claws, and they began practising for a concert they were going to perform at the hospital on Christmas Day.

"Got to get you and Ruth a coat for the winter," Birdie said, looking out at the snow. "Can't put it off no longer. Old man winter is here already, breathing up and down the coast."

"I'll help," Katie offered.

That evening, Birdie hauled out an old trunk crammed with coats, dresses, trousers, and odd bits of clothing. "I calls this me treasure chest," she said. "All this stuff was sent from Canada and the United States. And it still got a lot of wear. I cuts down the coats and dresses, and makes new clothes for the youngsters."

Katie didn't comment.

"When I gets finished," Birdie continued, "'tis as good as what yeh can buy anywheres. Even Dr. Grenfell says so." She picked up a silk dress from the trunk. It had a scalloped lace collar and lace sleeves.

"Will yeh look at that?" she laughed scornfully. "Them people from the mainland. Now who'd they think will wear that around here? Can you just picture some woman out on the mesh pickin' berries with that on?" She eyed the material critically. "Good to make doll's clothes, I s'pose. Everyt'ing comes in handy and I don't throw nothin' away."

Katie picked up a red coat from the pile. Her eye caught sight of another coat—one that was trimmed with white fur. "Could we make Ruth's coat from this one?"

"Well, sure we can." Birdie said.

Katie held up the other coat. "And can we use the fur off this coat to put on the collar?"

"Sounds like a grand idea," Birdie said. "I'll get to work on it straightaway."

She watched as Birdie's crooked fingers quickly ripped up the coats. She got needles, thimbles, and thread from her sewing basket. She handed them to Katie who broke as many as a dozen needles, and jabbed her fingers until they felt like pin cushions. But finally the two coats were finished, and now she looked at the work with pride. Ruth's coat looked like something that came straight out of the catalogue. Birdie is right, Katie thought. They're as good as you can buy anywhere.

An idea began taking shape in her mind. "Birdie," she said, "sometimes I sees coats like this in the catalogue. Sometimes they're as high as four . . . even five dollars. I could earn money for school by making and selling coats."

Birdie nodded. "You'll need money if yeh goes into nursing. I could give yeh a hand every now and then. Not 'til after Christmas though. Right now, I'm too busy making me presents. Not that many days left."

Christmas—the word hit Katie like a fist in the stomach. How could she spend Christmas without Mama and Papa and Hannah? She couldn't even imagine it.

The following day a letter came for Katie. It was postmarked St. John's, and she saw that her old address had been crossed out, and someone—it looked like Aunt Til's shaky handwriting— had written, *Children's Home, c/o Grenfell Mission, St. Anthony, St. Barbe's North.* Katie knew at once the letter was from Matt, and eagerly she tore it open.

> *Dear Katie,*
> *Hope this letter finds you well. I was not able to visit as planned, but have often thought of you. Bishop Field College is interesting. Half the teachers are British, the other half are*

Newfoundlanders. Most of the boys are the sons of Water Street merchants. A few, like myself, are not so well off. Some have won scholarships, or are being sponsored. I have made friends with one of the younger boys who, like myself, was sent here by an uncle. His name is Joey Smallwood, (we call him "Splits") and he really livens things up around here. Last week he led a protest in the cafeteria demanding, "More lassy, and less puddin'." He is a strange fellow, though, and spends all his free time at the visitors' gallery at the Newfoundland House of Assembly, which is three blocks from the school. I am planning a trip to Trinity Bay in early spring. I will drop into Fathom Harbour to see you. I will be thinking of you.

All the best,

Matt.

Tears pricked Katie's eyes. Matt didn't know what had happened to them. He didn't know Hannah wasn't with them anymore, that Ruth and Katie were in an orphanage. She got a pen and some paper and painfully she wrote her friend, explaining everything.

Days followed days, and before Katie knew it, it was the week before Christmas. The kitchen was filled with the wonderful smells of Birdie's homemade pies, cakes, and raisin bread. The children made decorations from colored paper and string. They decorated the sitting room with garlands of fir boughs and paper flowers. Miss Storr played the piano, and the children sang Christmas carols.

On Christmas Eve Birdie came out of the woods dragging a large pine tree, nearly three times her size. Katie went along with all of it. She sang Christmas carols with the younger children. She knitted scarves and mitts and vamps to give them for Christmas. She even hung up a stocking on Christmas Eve. But in her heart she knew Christmas would never be the same again.

Chapter 9

CHRISTMAS 19-13

*K*atie could smell sausage frying. Mmmm. It was not often they had sausage. *I hope Mama's made scrambled eggs too. When it comes to eggs, Mama makes the best.*

"Katie, wake up."

Her eyes fluttered open, and for a moment she focused on the faded wallpaper of her bedroom at the orphanage. She could see the homemade Christmas wreath Emily had placed in the window. From downstairs came the mingled sounds of chatter and laughter. Ruth was standing by her bed, cheeks flushed with excitement. "Look, Katie!" she said, holding up a loaded stocking. "Look what Sandy Claws left me."

Katie groaned. She wanted to go back to sleep.

"He left a stocking for you too. There's nuts and candy and . . ."

As much as Katie dreaded facing Christmas, she knew she had to get up for Ruth's sake. "I'll be right down," she promised, forcing a smile.

"Hurry," Ruth said, as she left the room. "We'll be opening the gifts soon."

Katie closed her eyes, images of Christmases past flooding her memory. She would awake early, the house smelling of apples and pine. Her father would have a fire going in the big woodstove while her mother bustled around the kitchen stuffing a goose or a duck. There would be bread pudding, and there would be potatoes, cabbage, turnip greens, and carrots, all boiling together in a big pot. Christmas was a time when there always seemed to be enough food.

They would attend a church service in the morning, and Katie's father would sing "The First Noel." Some people said it was worth going to church just to hear him sing. When they got home, gifts would be opened, and then they would eat Christmas dinner. Katie's heart squeezed with sadness, knowing they would never be a family again.

"Katie?" Birdie rapped sharply at the bedroom door. "Gonna come downstairs?" She opened the door and poked her head through. "We're all waitin' for yeh."

"I'll be right there, Birdie." Katie got out of bed and dressed quickly in the cold room. The windows were covered with frost, and her breath curled like smoke.

Downstairs, everyone was sitting around the tree waiting. "We are about to open our presents," Miss Storr said. She placed a generous number of gifts in front of Katie.

She opened the presents without enthusiasm. There was a knitted sweater from Miss Storr, and Birdie had made her a red velvet dress with lace on the collar. All the children had made something for her. There was a pink heart from Ruth, and a wooden whistle from Ben and Joseph. Emily had knitted her a pair of socks. The last gift she opened was from Aunt Til. It didn't have fancy wrappings like the other gifts, but was simply covered in newspaper and tied with red yarn. Inside Katie found a knitted sweater and a pair of mitts.

She smoothed out the many layers of newspaper. She would keep it to read later. There were no newspapers in St. Anthony, and even old news was a welcome treat.

For the next little while, the children proudly displayed pocket knives, dolls, games, and whistles. Ruth gleefully showed Katie a feather doll that had been left for her under the tree. Despite everything, she took delight in watching the younger children. After a while, they went into the dining room where Birdie served them toast, eggs, and orange juice. Katie wasn't hungry, but she managed to drink a cup of tea.

Before they had finished eating, someone shouted that Sandy Claws was walking across the frozen harbor. "And he got a bag of presents on his back," one little boy declared. Hearing this, some of the children jumped up from the table and ran for the door.

"Get back here and put yer coats on," Birdie yelled after them. "Yous'll all come down with pneumonia."

No one heard. With pigtails and shirttails flying, the children ran out into the cold winter morning. Minutes later, a half-frozen Santa was ushered into the children's home. His mustache was frozen solid, and icicles hung from his thick, white beard. After putting down the bag of gifts, he blew into his hands, rubbing them together for warmth.

"Come on in," Birdie said graciously. "Come on in, dear old Sandy Claws, and get yer old bones thawed out." She scrambled to make him a cup of hot tea while Miss Storr hung up his snowshoes.

"Just got back from th' Labrador," he told the children. "Had me breakfast in an igloo with an Eskimo family." He pointed to his bulging bag. "Their huskies tried to eat the presents. Managed to save some though." As he spoke, the younger children stared wide-eyed.

Sandy Claws reached into his bag and pulled out a gaily wrapped gift. "For Birdell," he said, reading the tag.

"More presents?" exclaimed Birdie. "Oh, Sandy Claws, Sandy Claws, how yeh spoils us." She reached eagerly for the gift, tore off the paper, uncovering a knitted shawl which she put around her neck, and then danced around the room.

As each gift emerged from Sandy Claws' sack, there were "ohs" and "ahs" from Birdie and the children.

By the time Katie went to the dinner table, she was feeling better. The hurt feeling she had when she first awoke had lessened. The delicious smell of stuffed partridge drifting from the oven lifted her spirits.

After dinner, she went up to her room, carrying the crumpled newspaper that had been wrapped around her gift from Aunt Til. Katie spread it out on her bed, smoothing the creased pages with her hand. The date across the top was *November 6, 1913*. On the first page was a story about two boys who accidentally burned down a barn while lighting a bonfire in honor of Guy Fawkes the evening before. On the next page, she read about the governor's wife serving tea at Government House. There was a photograph of her in a wide-brimmed hat and white gloves. But it was the photograph beneath it that caught and held Katie's attention. She gripped the newspaper with trembling hands. "No, it can't be," she said aloud. She read the short article again and again. *Mr. and Mrs. Silas Abbot have a new addition to their family. On a recent visit to Labrador, the couple returned with a fifteen-month-old orphan girl. The Abbotts, who have no children of their own, are planning to adopt the child.* Katie stared hard at the photograph. The Abbotts, she realized, were the people who came to Labrador during the summer. The photograph in the newspaper was one Mr. Abbott had taken of Hannah on the beach. Katie hugged the newspaper to her chest.

"Katie?" Miss Storr called. "Katie, it's nearly one-thirty."

She stood up quickly, remembering she had promised Birdie to help get the little ones ready for the Christmas concert at the hospital. She had become so absorbed in the newspaper article, it had completely slipped her mind. "I'll be right there," she called. Hastily, she shoved the newspaper under her mattress and went downstairs.

It was nearly two-thirty when they arrived at the hospital. Nurses, doctors, patients and staff had gathered on a ward where the beds had been pushed against the wall. A large tree had been set up and the room decorated with garlands of boughs.

For more than an hour Katie listened as the children delighted their audience with anthems, carols, recitations, and songs. The youngest child sang "Jingle Bells," and little Kirkina sang a hymn in her native language. When Ben did a skit about the cow that ate the Christmas tree, the audience roared. Then Ruth stood in the centre of the ward and sang "The First Noel." As Katie listened to her sister's clear, sweet voice, she felt her eyes moisten. It was as if Papa was with them. She thought of the newspaper hidden under her mattress. *We are a family,* she told herself. *We belong together.*

Chapter 10

FEBRUARY 1914

"And this one's for Katie," Miss Storr said, handing her a letter that came in the morning mail. Katie reached for it eagerly. She had been expecting a letter from Matt for some time now. As soon as she learned about Hannah's whereabouts, she had written her friend, asking him to look up the Abbotts' address in St. John's. However, a quick glance at the small, precise handwriting told her this letter was not from Matt, but from Gwen. The postmark showed it had been mailed on December 2, more than two months ago. Now, she wondered if Matt's letter had even reached him. Today was the first time in many weeks that the steamer could get into the harbor. Even now, it had to anchor half a mile out, and mail and freight had to be carried over the ice by dog team. At this time of the year, they were lucky to receive mail at all.

Katie turned her attention back to the letter in her hand.

> *Dear Katie,*
> *Thank-you for your last letter. I always enjoy the news from St.Anthony. Even here in Halifax, people have heard about the famous Dr.Grenfell and the Grenfell mission. Just yesterday, I bought his book,* Adrift on an Ice Pan.
>
> *Katie, I know you have gone as far as you possibly can with your schooling on the coast. I also know how much you want to be a nurse. I would like for you to come to Halifax to finish your education.*
>
> *After that, you could train at the Victoria General Hospital. I would love to have you live with me. Think about it, Katie, and get back to me.*
> *Love Gwen.*

With a resigned sigh, Katie shoved the letter into her sewing basket. *I wish I could, Gwen. I would like nothing better than to go to school in Halifax, but I have to find Hannah before I can do anything.* She closed the lid firmly and went back to the dress she was sewing. Since Christmas, Katie had spent all her spare time making coats and dresses. With the money she earned from this dress, she would have nearly thirty dollars saved. As soon as she had enough money, she would go to St. John's to look for Hannah. Only then could she think about finishing her education. Hannah and Ruth were what she lived for now, and the need to find Hannah motivated everything she did.

Chatter and laughter filled the hallway, and Katie knew Birdie was getting the children ready to go outside. Katie could hear her talking to them in a low voice as she helped them with their boots, coats, and scarves. "C'mon now, Harry. You're a big b'y. You knows how to put on yeh own coat. Leo, yeh better stop that right now. Yeh want to be left behind?"

A little while later, Birdie poked her head into the sitting room. "Why don't yeh put away all that sewin', Katie, and come with us? A nice walk'll do yeh a world of good."

She hesitated before putting her material aside. She was sewing a dress for Mrs. Patey's daughter's wedding, and she had promised to have it ready in a couple of days. Katie had been sewing for two days straight, and her fingers were stiff. She could use a break, she decided.

Carefully, she placed needles, thimbles, and thread inside her sewing basket, and went to join Birdie and the children.

"Peter won't be with us much longer," Birdie said, as she helped the two-year-old put on his boots. "Dr. Grenfell found a home for him in Boston."

"New Mama and Papa." Peter said proudly.

"Good for you, Peter," Katie told him, and the little boy gave her a wide smile, dimples deepening his rosy cheeks.

"I'll say this much for the doctor," Birdie said. "He always manages to find homes for the babies."

Katie knew only too well how Dr. Grenfell felt about babies being raised in orphanages. It was the reason she'd decided not to mention seeing Hannah's picture in the newspaper. Dr. Grenfell would most likely disapprove of her trying to get Hannah back. For all Katie knew, Birdie and Miss Storr might feel the same way. No, she decided, it was better to keep it to herself. She would wait until she found Hannah and let them know then.

Birdie held open the door while the little ones trudged single file out into the chilly afternoon. There was a slight breeze, and Katie felt snow swirl around her legs as she walked. Long icicles glistened like silver swords from the eaves of the mission buildings. Snow came almost to the tops of fences; it covered rooftops and the branches of trees.

"Look at them t'ings stickin' out of the ground," Birdie said, gesturing to a row of electric light poles and wires that ran through the woods. "Right ugly they is."

"Miss Storr says we're lucky to have electricity. Most places in Newfoundland don't have it." Katie remembered the kerosene lamps that had to be cleaned almost daily, their wicks cut and trimmed.

"I s'pose, girl."

They walked in silence until they reached a path leading into the woods; then Birdie turned to Katie. "Well," she said. "Yeh gonna go?"

"Go? Where to?"

Some of the children had gotten off the beaten path and were knee deep in the snow. "Don't yous wander off," Birdie called after them. She pulled a letter from her coat pocket. "Got this from Gwen this morning. Says she wrote you too. Says she wants you to go to Canada." Birdie gazed levelly at Katie.

"I'm goin' to St. John's," Katie told her. She didn't tell Birdie she planned to leave within the next couple of months.

Birdie shrugged. "Would be a good opportunity, I s'pose. But I understands how you feels. I wouldn't leave me country for anyt'ing." She shuddered. "And yeh never knows what they might do, them people from away. Look what happened to poor little Pomiuk."

Katie knew Birdie was referring to a boy from the Labrador who was brought to the Chicago world fair. Dr. Grenfell had told them the story many times. Pomiuk and his people were put on display in an Eskimo village at the fair. Many of them got sick. Pomiuk was sent back to Labrador with a broken leg that never healed properly.

"Some people will do anything for the ungodly dollar," Birdie said, tugging at her scarf. "'Tis no wonder so many people comes here. Must be good to be among people who's civilized."

They followed the path up over Fox Farm Hill and circled around until they came out behind the hospital. They passed houses built for people who worked for the mission. They were bigger than the other houses in St. Anthony. Standing apart from the others was a three-story house, newly built with a pitched roof and a glassed-in veranda. The house belonged to Dr. Grenfell, and although Katie had seen it many times, she gaped in awe. By the side door, a horse was hitched to a sleigh that was piled high with furniture. Two men were unloading a four-poster bed with ornately carved posts.

"High society is come to St. Anthony," Birdie said, clicking her tongue.

Katie followed her gaze to a fancy mahogany table and a sofa elaborately upholstered in fine brocade. She knew Mrs. Grenfell was always ordering dishes and furniture. Every time the steamer arrived, there was something for her.

"I hear the house is beautiful inside," Katie said. "Miss Storr says it's got all kinds of modern appliances, steam heat, and indoor plumbing."

"A pity they don't stay home long enough to enjoy it," Birdie snapped.

"They are away quite a bit," Katie agreed.

"I hear Mrs. Grenfell is right stuck-up." Birdie sniffed. "Don't know what I'll feed that one when she comes for dinner. Dare say she'll be too proud to eat the same grub as we. The doctor, now, he'll eat anything yeh puts in front of him."

"Mrs. Grenfell's comin' for dinner? When?"

"She's away now," Birdie explained. "Her and the two youngsters is visiting her parents in the States. Won't be back 'til sometime in the spring."

"But Birdie, why didn't you tell me she was comin' to visit?"

Birdie shrugged. "Must have slipped me mind, girl."

"Will the children be coming with her?" Katie asked, thinking of the Grenfells' two little boys, three-year-old Wilfred and one-year-old Kinlock.

Birdie snorted. "I dare say they'll stay home with the governess. A *governess,* mind yeh. From *England.*" She shoved her hands in her pockets. "Got her own cook too."

"Horsies," Peter shouted. He pointed to some animals that had come out of the woods and were standing on the path. They were the size of small horses and the color of molasses. They came fearlessly up to the children, sniffing the air.

"They're reindeer," Katie told the little boy. She knew that Dr. Grenfell had three hundred of them shipped from Lapland. They had become a common sight around the hospital grounds.

Not far behind the reindeer were a man and woman and a young boy. They were dressed in colorful knee length coats made from scraps of material. The man and boy wore deerskin trousers and high, four-cornered caps, the woman a close-fitting hood. The man had a sheath knife and tobacco pouch hanging from his belt. Katie had first seen them from the windows of the hospital, and Gwen had explained that they were Laplanders. They had come to St. Anthony to teach the local people how to herd and take care of the reindeer. They nodded and smiled at the children as they passed.

"The doctor's reindeer," Birdie said scornfully. "Useless as an udder on a bull, they is."

"Not completely useless," Katie said.

"No, I s'pose not," Birdie said somewhat grudgingly. "They gives us milk and cheese. But the doctor t'ought they would replace the huskies for travel." She cackled. "S'pose he t'ought they was gonna fly over the snow like Sandy Claws' reindeer." Birdie pulled the collar of her coat up to her ears. "Sometimes, I thinks the doctor gets all his fancy notions from that Yankee wife of his."

Katie was only half listening. Her thoughts were on Anne Grenfell. She had only seen the doctor's wife from a distance. She wore stylish coats and hats. And now, Katie was finally going to meet this very interesting woman.

Chapter 11

APRIL 1914

It was the middle of April before the Grenfells got around to visiting the children's home. Katie could feel her spirits lifting that morning as she sat in the parlor sewing. Winter had finally released its grip, and the harbor ice was breaking up and drifting through the narrows. The window stood open to a light spring breeze, bringing with it a heavy moist scent of melting snow and ice. Boats, paddles, and lobster pots that had been snowed under for months were now visible, and she could see dark patches of earth in the yard. Miss Storr had discarded her sealskin coat for one of a lighter material and had put away her winter boots in favour of her "Wellington" boots. The sun had licked at the icicles until they were as thin as knitting needles, and everywhere was the drip, drip, dripping of spring.

Katie wrestled with an important decision. She wanted to leave the children's home by the end of May or the first week in June. She wondered now, if it would be better to leave her sister at the children's home while she went searching for Hannah. It would only be for a brief time, she told herself. Still, she worried how Ruth would feel. The child had lost her mother and father. Katie didn't want her to think she was being abandoned. She would have to talk with her sister, make her understand how important it was that they all be together.

In the kitchen, she could hear Birdie bustling about getting things ready for the Grenfells' visit. They were expected to arrive any minute now, and every child in the orphanage was eagerly waiting for them. Birdie had taken down all the good china and had covered the dining room table with a fine lace tablecloth. "Now don't none of yous go gawkin'," she drilled the younger children. "I don't want Mrs. Grenfell goin' back to the States tellin' everybody about the brazen orphans she seen in Newfoundland. And Ben, we'll have none of your foolish remarks today. No nonsense, yeh hear."

Putting down her sewing, Katie got up and went into the kitchen to see if Birdie needed help. The counter was lined with trays and platters of food. Miss

Storr had made egg salad and lobster sandwiches and a salad from asparagus and tinned tomatoes. Birdie had baked cakes and cookies, and two raspberry pies were still cooling on the table.

Katie put on an apron, rolled up her sleeves and began clearing away pans and bowls. She worked steadily, listening to Birdie grumble. "All this fuss. I'm sure the doctor wouldn't mind if we served him boiled cod heads."

"They're here!" Kirkina shouted after a while. She and Ruth had been sitting by the window for most of the morning, noses pressed against the glass.

Katie went to the window to take a look. Birdie wiped her hands on her apron and went to stand beside her. "Good Lord!" she exclaimed, as she watched Dr. Grenfell open the garden gate. "I wonder where the doctor thinks he's goin' to dressed like that?"

Katie smiled, taking in the doctor's three-piece suit and a top hat. They were not used to seeing him in such a getup. He usually wore odd socks, baggy pants, and old sweaters with holes. Miss Storr once told them how he received an award from some university wearing odd shoes.

Ruth ran out into the sitting room. Katie and Birdie followed. Miss Storr greeted the Grenfells at the door. The little ones, who always ran to the doctor, now hung back. They stared at Mrs. Grenfell with eyes as big as soup bowls. Katie thought she looked elegant in a pale green dress and a large hat decorated with flowers and feathers.

Birdie looked Dr. Grenfell up and down.

"Anne says I should dress more like an English gentleman," he said, sheepishly.

Miss Storr smiled. Birdie sniffed her disapproval. Anne took off her hat, showing off her hair that was pinned back in an elaborate twist. "Everything is so beautiful," she exclaimed, taking in the homemade paper flowers and the fancy dishes that had been laid out.

She went around the room, talking to the children, asking their names, and patting their heads as if they were pets. Katie found it hard not to stare at her.

"How was your trip to England?" Miss Storr asked politely, after everyone had been seated around the table. The children had grown very quiet, their gaze fixed on Mrs. Grenfell.

"Oh, we've had *so* many thrilling experiences," she exclaimed. "And we have met *so* many important people." She took a sip of tea and put the cup down gingerly on its saucer. "We had lunch with the famous explorer, Sir Ernest Shackleton, and Count Marconi came to see us at our hotel. Count Marconi gave the *Strathcona* her wireless installation, you see. And King George himself sent for Wilf." She nodded toward Dr. Grenfell. "They chatted for nearly an hour."

Birdie sniffed audibly but said nothing. She continued to pour tea into delicate cup that were decorated with roses and violets.

Mrs. Grenfell talked all through lunch. "Wilf and I will be returning to England again in the fall. I'm afraid your Newfoundland winters are much too cold for us." She pronounced it "New-Found-Land," enunciating each syllable as if they were three separate words. Katie saw some of the younger children cover their mouths to hide their laughter.

"Of course, Wilf is becoming quite famous, and . . ."

"Katie here is goin' away to be a nurse," Birdie said, deliberately interrupting her. "For months now, she's been makin' and sellin' coats and dresses and savin' up all her money."

Everyone's attention was now on Katie.

"A nurse is very useful," Mrs. Grenfell said.

Dr. Grenfell smiled his approval. "We always need nurses along our coast, Kate."

Katie nodded.

"Gwen is after her to go to Canada," Birdie said. "But she's got her mind set on St. John's."

"There are more opportunities in Canada," said Mrs. Grenfell. "The Victoria General Hospital is an excellent place to train. And you will have Gwen giving you the support you need."

"A lad from Labrador is thinking about going to Harvard Medical," said Dr. Grenfell. "If you would like to go to school in Halifax, we could have it arranged by September."

"Thank-you," Katie said, quietly.

They ate in silence for a few moments, and then Dr. Grenfell launched into a discussion about the seal hunt. From listening to the conversation, Katie learned that more than a hundred men had perished this season. Because the doctor had a wireless, he often got news before anyone else. "It's the greed of the ship owners," he said grimly. "They refuse to provide adequate clothing or even equipment for the men's safety."

Katie recalled stories her father used to tell when he came back from seal hunting. For weeks the men lived on nothing but hard tack and tea. Sometimes there would be no drinking water.

Once he and four other men were stranded on a drifting ice floe during a blizzard. They were rescued after eighteen hours. One man had perished while another had lost a foot to frostbite.

"The price of seal pelts is considered to be far more important than a man's life," Dr. Grenfell said, breaking into Katie's thoughts.

The younger children had lost interest in the conversation at this point and had turned their attention to eating.

After the Grenfells left, Birdie mimicked Mrs. Grenfell's soft, refined voice. "*King George himself sent for Wilf* . . . I tell yeh, that woman is gonna have the doctor as stuck-up as she is her own self. And did yeh see that ridiculous lookin' outfit he was wearin'?" She jerked to her feet, and began stacking plates and gathering cutlery. "King George!"

Chapter 12

MAY 1914

"Yeh got a visitor," Bertie told Katie early one morning. They had just finished breakfast, and she was helping Ruth wash the dishes.

"A visitor?" Katie wiped her hands on her apron. "For me?"

"He's outside in the garden. I asked him to come in, but he says he'll wait for yeh there."

He? Who could be visiting her at the children's home? Katie quickly pulled off her apron and smoothed back wisps of hair from her face. She put on a cardigan, and hurried outside. The sun was shining, the birds twittered in the low branches of the trees, and the sounds of spring were all around her. Mud was drying in the rutted footpaths outside the fence. The ground was covered with yellow dandelions— "bumblebee flowers," the children called them. Daisies and buttercups bloomed near the garden fence. A

Savannah sparrow darted swiftly across the yard, eyeing Katie with interest.

A tall man wearing a gray sweater was standing by the fence looking out at the ocean. Although Katie couldn't see his face, there was something vaguely familiar about him.

"Sir?"

Hearing Katie's voice, he turned quickly, his eyes lighting up at the sight of her.

Katie let out a little gasp of surprise. "Matt?" She whispered. "Where did you come from?"

He reached for Katie's hands, and held them in his own. Katie was aware of how he towered over her. At that moment, the Savannah sparrow began to sing.

"We're on our way to the Labrador," Matt explained. "The skipper of the *Shanaditti* gave us passage. He had to drop off supplies here at St. Anthony. I won't be fishin' this summer. I'm be helpin' Uncle Henry run the cooperative store in Red Bay."

"Did . . . did . . . ?

"I got your letter," Matt said gently, before she could finish. "When I found out we had to stop off here, I decided to deliver the news in person."

Katie nodded, impatient to hear what he had to say.

"We don't have much time," he said. "Perhaps yeh could walk down to the wharf with me. We'll talk on the way." He turned onto a narrow footpath that led to the wharf. Katie followed him like a hungry puppy that had been promised food.

"I looked up the Abbotts' address in the telephone directory," Matt said after a while. "I even went to their house on Circular Drive."

Katie's heart quickened as she waited for Matt to continue.

"There was a *For Sale* sign on the lawn. I talked to some of the neighbors, and they told me the Abbotts moved to Canada—to Halifax. I tried to get their address, but nobody had it."

Katie sank down on a broken fence post.

"You okay?" Matt asked, sitting down beside her.

She nodded. "It's just that I . . . I didn't expect this."

"I'm sorry, Katie. I know it must come as a shock." He peered at her closely. "What will you do now?"

She told Matt she had been saving her money. She told him about Gwen inviting her to go to Canada. "There's only one thing I can do," she said, her voice filled with determination. "I'm going to Halifax to look for Hannah."

Matt frowned. "What will you say to the Abbotts? I don't know if yeh can just waltz in there, and take Hannah from them."

Katie rose to her feet. "I have to get her back. We're family." She sighed. "Problem is, I may have to leave Ruth in the children's home while I'm gone."

"Is that a big problem?" Matt asked.

"I'll miss her, of course. And I'm sure she'll miss me. But Matt, I promised our mother that I would take care of my sisters."

Matt was thoughtful. "Are they taking good care of Ruthie at the children's home?"

"Well, yes—and she seems happy."

"My grandmother used to say that sometimes the decisions we make may not be the best for one family member, but we have to do what is best for everyone."

"Hannah is as much Ruth's sister as she is mine," Katie said, thoughtfully. "I knows she misses her as much as I do."

"Why don't you talk to Ruth and find out how she feels about being left in the children's home," Matt suggested.

They were approaching the wharf now where men were unloading freight from the boat.

"That's our boat there," Matt said, pointing to a small vessel with *Shanaditti* written on her side.

There were other boats in the harbor, their towering colorful sails billowing in the morning breeze. Chains clanked loudly as barrels of flour and tubs of butter and salt beef were thrown in a heap on the wharf. A short man with a ruddy face was shouting orders to men and boys in rubber boots.

"That's Uncle Henry," Matt said, a slight smile touching his lips. "The way he orders people around, you'd think he was the skipper instead of a paying passenger."

The man saw Katie and Matt and began to approach them.

"Uncle Henry, this is my friend, Katie Andrews."

Katie held out her hand. "Pleased to meet yeh, sir."

Uncle Henry grasped Katie's hand. "The nephew said he was goin' to visit a girl. I thought 'twas all a sham to get out of helping with the unloading." He winked at Matt. "Never told us how pretty yeh was. Can't say I blames him for rushin' off the minute we landed."

Katie could feel herself blushing. Matt reached for her hand, and gave it a little squeeze.

"All aboard," someone shouted from the deck. A man began to untie the ship's ropes.

"Better get movin', my son," Uncle Henry told Matt. Katie saw that most of the men were already making their way up the gangplank. Matt put his arm around Katie's shoulders.

"Write to me, Katie," he said. "Let me know how yeh makes out."

"Good-bye, Matt," she whispered as she watched him walk up the gangplank behind Uncle Henry.

Katie watched as the *Shanaditti* moved away from the wharf. Gulls circled the water, screeching and fighting for scraps of fish. She waved until the boat was out of sight, then walked slowly back to the children's home.

In her room, she took Gwen's letter from her sewing basket and reread it.

Katie knew what she had to do. She would go to Halifax as Dr. and Mrs. Grenfell suggested. Dr. Grenfell told her about a school in Halifax that he would arrange for her to attend. But she knew it could take weeks—months even—to find Hannah. Could she leave Ruth for such a long stretch of time? She would have to talk to Ruth, make her understand.

After lunch, Katie called her sister into the library. "Ruth," she began. "Are yeh happy here?"

The little girl nodded. "This is where my friends is to. And Birdie and Miss Storr."

Katie smiled at her. "Do you remember when Hannah used to live with us?"

A look of sadness flickered across Ruth's face. "Yes, and I remembers Mama and Papa. And I remembers the house we used to live in." She looked at Katie. "Can we go back there sometime?"

Katie shook her head. "Not now, Ruthie. But we may be able to get Hannah back again. Would yeh like that?"

Ruth nodded eagerly. "When?"

"Well, she's in Canada right now. And that's what I wants to talk with you about." Katie swallowed. "I need to go there to find her. But while I'm gone, Ruth, would yeh mind staying here?"

"Will yeh come back again?" Ruth asked anxiously.

"Of course, I'll come back." Katie put her arms around her younger sister and held her tight. "I'll come back as soon as I finds Hannah, I promise."

"Will yeh be gone for a long time?"

Katie felt a pang of sadness. She knew that even weeks would seem like a long time to someone as young as her sister. "Maybe," she said. "Yeh see, Ruthie, I don't know where Hannah is to. It might take some time to find her. But I will write every day, I promise."

"Okay," Ruth said, cautiously.

Katie could tell her sister was putting on a brave front and it tore at her heart. Ruth had barely said a word about Mama's and Papa's deaths. At times, it was hard to tell what she was feeling.

That night Katie lay awake for a long time. It will only be for a little while, she told herself. And like Matt said, I'm leaving Ruth in the hands of good people. Yet she tossed and turned.

She recalled how quiet Ruth had been during supper that evening. She barely touched her food. When the other children gathered around Miss Storr at the piano, Ruth went to her room. Later, Katie found her sitting on her bed, her hands tucked under her chin.

The next morning, when Katie went down to the kitchen, Birdie was kneading dough in a large ceramic bowl. There was a smudge of flour on her face. Six pie pans were greased and spread out on the counter.

"Well, well, look what th' cat dragged in," she said when she saw Katie.

Katie sat down heavily in a chair.

"Well," Birdie said, after a moment. "Looks like yeh got a lot on yeh mind."

"I've come to a decision," Katie said.

"Oh?" Birdie had rolled out the dough and was now concentrating on fitting it over the top of one of the pie plates.

Katie rose up from the chair and went to stand by the window. "I've decided to take Gwen up on her offer and go to school in Canada."

"Well, I s'pose 'tis your life," Birdie said. She reached for a knife and began trimming the excess dough from around the pies. "More opportunities in Canada, like Mrs. Grenfell said. And Gwen'll be there. Not like you'll be on yeh own."

For a brief moment, Katie considered confiding in Birdie. She and Birdie had become friends, and Katie felt a stab of guilt not being completely honest with her. But how would Birdie feel about Katie's decision? Would she try to discourage her? Time enough to tell her when I find Hannah, she reasoned.

"Birdie, do you think Ruth will be okay if I leaves her here?"

"We'll take good care of Ruth," Bertie said. "No need to uproot her when she's doin' so well." She looked at Katie. "Besides, it'll be months before you moves away."

Katie nodded, but there was a heaviness in her chest as she walked away.

PART II

Chapter 13

JULY 1914

$\mathcal{I}$t was a late Sunday afternoon when Katie arrived in Halifax. Anxiously, she scanned the dock, looking for Gwen who had promised to meet her. Katie had gone through Customs and Immigration, and now there was nothing to do but stroll idly about. From the wharf, she could see the railroad, piers, and factories, the docks with their vast warehouses. She could hear the clang of steel and the creak of wood as cargo was unloaded. Dockworkers moved busily about, lifting and wheeling, loading and unloading, staggering under the heavy weight of sacks and bales.

Men and women hurried by with bags and suitcases, the men wearing tall brimmed hats and suits with heavy watch chains draped across the front. A few carried walking canes, elaborately trimmed with silver or gold. The women wore large decorative hats and skirts with calf-high slits. Some carried babies in their arms, or held small children by the hand. Katie imagined Hannah getting off the boat with Mrs. Abbott. Whenever she thought of Hannah, she imagined her holding the wooden doll their father had made for her.

The moist, salty air filled Katie's nostrils, and the many schooners and vessels in the harbor reminded her of her days on the Labrador. She looked around at the black smoke from the many factories in the area. The city was grimy and dirty, not quite what she expected. She imagined more grass and trees. In one of her letters, Gwen had written that there were trams, telephones, and movie theaters. But Katie knew her purpose for coming to Canada was to find Hannah.

"Katie?"

Hearing her name, she reeled around to find Gwen. She hugged Katie hard. "I'm sorry I wasn't here when your boat arrived," she said. "There was an emergency at the hospital. Look at you," she said, admiringly. "You've grown up."

Katie smiled. Gwen's blonde hair was longer and held back by bobby pins, but she looked exactly as Katie remembered her.

"Come," Gwen said, "the cab is waiting." She led Katie away from the wharf and into a narrow cobblestone street where a man in a tweed suit was standing by a horse and buggy. Without a word, he took Katie's suitcase and helped her up onto a high-perched seat. Once everyone was settled, he pulled the reins. The horse moved forward, steel-rimmed wheels rattling over cobblestones.

"When we get home, I want to hear all the news from Newfoundland," Gwen said.

Katie nodded, but she had very little to say at that moment. Tall buildings stretched upward, some of them five and six stories high. She turned her head in every direction, not wanting to miss anything. Never before had she seen so many people in one place. Streets and alleyways sloped upward from the water-front, and in some places they were very steep. As the buggy rolled on, Katie was surprised to see that some of the sidewalks were made of brick. The stores and houses were so close together, they looked as if they were joined. They drove slowly, the clip-clopping of the horse's feet echoing through the streets. Sidewalks were lined with stores and cafés with colorful striped awnings. Mannequins in store windows displayed dresses, hats, coats, and men's suits. A motorcar passed by, honking its horn. Katie stared, dumbfounded. She had heard of such things, of course, but she had only seen them in the magazines Mrs. Grenfell brought to the children's home.

Along the way, Gwen pointed out places of interest. "That's Citadel Hill," she said, gesturing toward a grassy slope high above the city. "And that's St. Paul's Cathedral next to the Grande Parade." The horse and buggy turned up a street with a large brick church on the corner. "We are now on Spring Garden Road," Gwen said.

Katie thought of flowers and running water. They passed houses with bay windows, domed turrets, fish scale shingles, and elaborately scrolled buttresses.

After a while, Gwen pointed to a high, black, wrought iron gate to the left of them. "Over there are the Public Gardens, one of the loveliest spots in Halifax," she said.

At that moment, a long shiny red vehicle came speeding around the corner. Katie was so startled, she rose abruptly to her feet. "Katie, do be careful," Gwen said. "A streetcar," she explained. "You'll get to ride one before you return to Newfoundland."

Katie drank everything in. In her mind, she composed letters to Birdie and Ruth, telling them about her adventure. She knew Ruth especially would like to hear about the trams, the busy streets, and tall buildings.

A little while later, the horse turned onto a pretty, tree-lined street with tidy rows of houses. The sign said *Summer Street,* and Katie knew it was Gwen's address from the countless letters she had sent to the children's home. She felt awed by the large houses, some with turrets and balconies jutting out over the street. The horse stopped in front of a house with a fancy arched doorway. It was nearly as large as the orphanage in St. Anthony and had bay windows decorated with sculptured garlands.

"You live here?" Katie asked. "In this big house?"

Gwen laughed. "Yes. I live in this big house, along with four other families. My flat is on the top floor." She paid the driver, picked up Katie's suitcase, and led her into the foyer and up a flight of stairs. Gwen unlocked the door, and ushered Katie into a comfortable room with a high ceiling and brick fireplace. There were soft, cosy armchairs and shelves filled with books. On the wall were framed photographs and paintings of landscapes.

Later, when they were sitting on the balcony drinking tea and eating blueberry scones, Katie told Gwen about her trip. There had been a singer from New York who sang for the passengers while Katie ate her meals in a fancy dining room with long tables draped in white linen. She talked with elegant ladies who told her of their travels to faraway places. She told Gwen all this while chords of "I'm Always Chasing Rainbows" played on a gramophone in the background.

Katie felt contented. She looked out over the tops of the maple trees, and down into backyards. Somewhere nearby, a bird was trilling. *Hannah is out there somewhere. It won't be long before I find her.*

Chapter 14

SEARCHING FOR HANNAH

*K*atie stared at the unfamiliar ceiling, the flowered wallpaper, and the white lace curtains that hung from tall windows. She rubbed her eyes, taking a moment to orient herself. For most of the night, she had lain awake in the darkness, thoughts tumbling around in her mind like bees in a bottle. The first light of dawn was pressing against her window when she finally dozed off.

She lay quietly listening as the muted sounds of early morning drifted up from the street below. Somewhere far off, she could hear a trolley coach. She could hear the echoing of horses' hoofs on the street as the milkman made his morning deliveries. Somewhere a dog was barking.

Fragments of a dream came back to her, filling her memory. She had been in a panic because she left Hannah on the ship. But as the ship sailed out to sea, it was Ruth, not Hannah, who lifted her hand in a final farewell. Now, Katie's stomach twisted painfully at the recollection of the dream. Did she make the right decision leaving Ruth at the children's home? It was something she had agonized over for months.

Katie got out of bed and put on the dress Birdie made her as a going away gift. It was dark brown with a white collar and white sleeves. As she adjusted the belt and methodically did up the buttons, she stared at herself in the mirror. Her face was pale, her eyes puffy. She brushed her curly hair, tying it back with a white ribbon. Gwen was still asleep. In the afternoon she was going to take Katie shopping, but this morning Katie had plans of her own. After filling the kettle, she picked up *McAlpine's City Directory* that rested on a table next to the telephone. Matt had found the Abbotts' address in the city directory in St. John's, and now Katie was hoping to find their address in Halifax.

She made herself a cup of tea and sat at the kitchen table with the directory on her lap. Abbots were listed on the very first page. Katie ran her finger down the long columns, silently reading the names. *Samuel, Sean, Sheldon, Sherman, Simon, Stedman, Sylvester . . .* there was no Silas listed. There was, however, S. R. Abbott on Quinpool Road, S. A. Abbott on Tobin

Street, and S. J. Abbott on Brenton Street. She found a
pen and jotted down the addresses.

Katie left the house at eight-thirty, walked to the
end of Summer Street and turned down Spring
Garden Road. She was unprepared for the noise and
the bustle. The sidewalks were already filling up, and
people hurried past her in both directions. There
seemed to be twice as many people on this Monday
morning as there were the afternoon before. From all
around her came the sounds of whinnying horses,
carriages, buggies, and automobiles. Men in three-
piece suits carried fancy cases while others in overalls
swung lunch pails at their side. Most of the women
wore dark clothing and sturdy shoes. Some nodded
and smiled at Katie; others hurried by without a
glance. Katie wandered along, her heart pounding.
She was uneasy being in such a big city with so many
people; yet at the same time she felt a growing excitement. She took note of the street names, knowing it
would be easy to get lost in a city this size.

After walking a couple of blocks, Katie stopped a
kindly looking lady and shyly asked for directions.
Twenty minutes later, she stood in front of a large
house on the corner of Quinpool Road and Beech
Street. She rang the doorbell, her palms clammy, her
legs threatening to buckle. Was Hannah inside?

A middle-aged woman opened the door.

"I'm looking for a Mr. Silas Abbott," Katie told her.

The woman smiled. "I'm sorry, my dear—my husband's name is Shamus. Shamus Abbott."

"Shamus?" Katie repeated, feeling a stab of disappointment.

The woman held the door open, as if uncertain of what to say next.

"Thank-you," Katie said, and she turned and walked away.

The house on Tobin Street was so run-down that before she even inquired of the people who lived inside, Katie decided it was not a place the Abbotts were likely to live. The names of the tenants were listed in the hallway, and she saw that there was a Sylvia Abbott in room #3. Katie didn't even bother to ring the bell.

By the time she reached Breton Street, the sun was high overhead. Feeling hot and tired, she took off her sweater and tucked it under her arm. The street was not very long, and in no time she found the house she was looking for, a two-story semidetached. She knocked on the door, but got no answer. She waited a couple of minutes, and was about to leave when she saw a lady with a bag of groceries coming down the street. She was a large woman, and she panted from the heat and the exertion of her heavy load. She stopped in front of the house that was attached to S. J. Abbott's and put the groceries on the sidewalk while she retrieved a key from her purse. She glanced curiously at Katie, but said nothing.

"Could you tell me who your neighbors are?" Katie asked. "They don't seem to be home."

"That's probably because they're away," the woman replied tartly.

"What are their names?"

"The Abbotts," the woman said, fitting the key in the door.

"Silas Abbott?" Katie asked eagerly.

The woman eyed her suspiciously. "No Silas here, only Stanley and Suzie."

Katie felt her heart sink. Waves of disappointment engulfed her. How would she ever find Hannah if she didn't know the Abbotts' address? There was nothing to do except go back to the flat. Gwen would probably be up by now, and she'd be expecting her for lunch. She walked to the end of Breton and turned right onto Spring Garden Road, her spirits low. Outside a tobacco shop, a boy was selling newspapers. "War is imminent," he cried. "Read all about it."

Katie remembered talk of war among the passengers on the ship. They referred to it as "the situation in

Europe," and they were afraid it might "escalate into a World War." Katie wondered how events so far away could affect the lives of people living in Newfoundland and Canada.

That afternoon, Gwen and Katie took a tram to Barrington Street. She bought a hat at Eaton's, marveling that she could buy so many things in one place. In St. Anthony, people had to order most things from the catalogue. In winter, it could take months to arrive. Here, you could buy everything from nylon stocking to electric stoves. And how different the stores were from the one in St. Anthony with its pot-bellied stove, barrels filled with salt beef and herring, and its wooden counter lined with jars of peppermints and other penny candies. Katie enjoyed walking up and down the streets, looking in store windows at the displays and the mannequins dressed in colorful clothes.

Afterwards, Gwen showed her the Halifax Academy, a large brick building that stood across from Citadel Hill. "They place great emphasis on the classics, "she told Katie. "A public examination is held annually."

Katie felt a stab of gratitude as she gazed at the fancy arched doorways and windows. Dr. Grenfell had arranged for her to attend this school. She realized that not everyone was given the same opportunity. She didn't even have to pass tenth grade to get into nursing. She had only to complete it. Katie knew though that she could not forget the real reason she came to Halifax. Once she found Hannah, she might not be able to continue her studies. But, as Birdie would say: "I'll leap over that puddle when I comes to it."

Katie followed Gwen down Queen Street, and they turned right on University Avenue. "That's where I work," she said, pointing to a long two-story brick building in the distance.

"The Victoria General Hospital." Katie said, breathlessly. As she got closer, she could see a balcony over the main entrance. Outside the front doors, a horse was hitched to a cart with *Victoria General Hospital* printed in black letters on the side.

"Would you like to go inside?" Gwen asked, and Katie nodded eagerly.

As they walked through the hospital's main doors, she felt a flutter of excitement. Is it possible, she wondered? Could she become a nurse someday? Gwen led her down a long narrow corridor. Katie breathed in the sharp, clean hospital smell. The tiles on the floor gleamed like mirrors, and doctors in white coats hurried by looking busy and important. Nurses in starched white uniforms wheeled patients in wooden roller chairs. Others balanced trays filled with pills and medicine.

Gwen showed her the chapel and the cafeteria, then took her to see the ward where she worked. She introduced her to some of the nurses, explaining that Katie planned to be a nurse someday. She felt a surge of excitement as if talking about it could make it all come true.

As they were leaving the ward, Katie almost collided with a big woman with a black cape draped around her shoulders. She wore black stockings and black lace-up shoes.

"Hello, Matron," Gwen greeted warmly, but the woman remained unsmiling.

"This is nurse Marshall," Gwen said, turning to Katie, "the matron on my ward."

"How do yeh do?" Katie held out her hand, and the matron took it, still unsmiling.

"I was showing Katie around," Gwen explained. "She wants to be a nurse, and she plans to do her training at this hospital."

The woman eyed Katie critically. "We can tell in three months if you will be any good or not." She gave her a tight, cynical smile. "We demand high standards from our student trainees. You have to be tough, and a lot of young girls just don't make it."

Katie felt her spirits droop.

Gwen put a reassuring arm on her shoulder. She leaned forward, her voice low. "You'll do just fine, Katie," she said encouragingly.

Chapter 15

AUGUST 1914

"This is considered to be the finest formal Victorian garden anywhere," Gwen said, pushing open the wrought iron gates to the Public Gardens. Katie followed her down a twisted gravel path past three statues of stone goddesses that stood in the central path. She looked around her, taking in her surroundings. There were grassy knolls, curved stone bridges, fountains, manicured flowerbeds, a duck pond, and every kind of flower imaginable. They found a stone bench near a cascading fountain on which a cherub was riding a leaping fish. Birds chirped in a grove of trees nearby.

Katie watched as a woman and two little boys threw breadcrumbs to the ducks, geese, and swans gathered at the edge of the pond. Did the Abbotts bring Hannah here? Thinking about her sister made Katie's heart leap with sadness.

"Of all the places in Halifax, this is the most beautiful," Gwen said. "And to think it was all converted from a swampland blueberry barren." She pointed to the center of the garden. "That Victorian bandstand over there was built about thirty years ago."

Katie was barely listening, her thoughts still on Hannah. There must be a way for her to get the Abbotts' address.

"Gwen," she said, after a while. "Do all people in Halifax have their telephone numbers listed?"

Gwen was thoughtful. "No. Not everyone. Some people may have moved to the city after the directory was published. They may have been too late to get their names in the book."

Of course, Katie thought. Why hadn't she thought of that?

"How can yeh get the number if it's *not* listed?"

"You could try calling the operator." Gwen looked quizzically at Katie. "Are you looking for someone?"

"It's something I've wondered about," she said evasively.

⌇

Katie learned that she could get the operator simply by dialing 0. However, it wasn't until the following day that she had a chance to make the call. Her hands trembled as she picked up the heavy black receiver.

"Can I help you?" Unprepared for the loud, clear voice that came over the wires, Katie was so startled it took her a moment to find her voice.

"I . . . I'm . . . lookin' for the telephone number for a Mr. Abbott. Mr. Silas Abbott," she amended, her heart pounding.

"One moment, please."

Katie waited anxiously.

After a few moments, the operator came back on the line. "I'm sorry," she said, "but we do not have a listing for Silas Abbott."

"You don't?"

"I'm afraid not."

"But . . . but . . ."

"I'm sorry, I cannot help you," the operator said.

Before Katie could say anything else, there was a loud click and a dial tone buzzing in her ear.

What am I to do now? I have to get in touch with them, or I will never find Hannah.

Katie suddenly felt tired. She went into the bedroom, closed the door, and lay down on her bed, disappointment weighing her down like an anchor.

She must have dozed off, because when she awoke the room was dark. She could see a crack of light under her door.

Rubbing sleep from her eyes, Katie walked down the hallway to the living room.

Gwen was sitting in a chair reading the newspaper. Her face was grim, but when she saw Katie she looked up and smiled. "Well, hello." she said. She folded the newspaper on her lap, but not before Katie had a chance to read the headlines. *World Panic-Stricken. Europe Faced With The Greatest Catastrophe In History, Is Sick With Anxiety And Fear.* Every day now, it seemed, the newspaper's headlines warned of war.

"Are you worried about a war starting?" Katie asked. She looked at the folded newspaper.

Gwen frowned. "Yes," she admitted. "I'm worried that Britain will be drawn into the war."

Katie was silent, thinking of Gwen's friends in England.

"Most Canadians do not think this situation will affect them," Gwen continued on. "But Canada is part of the empire. Sir Wilfred Laurier was right when he said that when Britain is at war, Canada is at war." She glanced toward the window, talking more to herself than to Katie. "If Britain becomes involved in this war, there could be serious consequences. It could be disastrous."

Katie had never seen Gwen this worried and it made her uneasy.

"Anyway," Gwen said, putting down the paper, "enough talk about war. I have to write a letter to my friend back in St. Anthony. Katie, would you mind getting me some stationery from the drawer in my secretarial?"

Katie went over to the mahogany desk and opened the drawer. The stationery Gwen had requested lay on top of a framed picture of a young girl. Katie took it out of the drawer and looked at it. At first, she thought it was a photograph of Gwen. But the girl's hair in this picture was much darker. "Who is she?" Katie asked, holding up the picture.

"It's my sister," Gwen said, rising abruptly to her feet. She took the picture from Katie's hands and without another word put it back in the drawer.

She was puzzled by Gwen's behavior and even more baffled that she had a sister. Once when Katie had asked Gwen about her family, she told her that her mother and father had died. She never mentioned a sister. Katie wanted to know more, but from the determined way Gwen closed the drawer, she knew there would be no more discussion on the subject. Was

Gwen's sister dead too? Katie recalled the sad, faraway look Gwen got whenever Katie mentioned Hannah or Ruth.

⌒

People all over the city seemed occupied with the threat of war. They talked about it when Katie went to the corner store to pick up groceries. There was talk of war while she waited for the tram. Then, on August 4, less than three weeks after Katie arrived in Halifax, Gwen came home from the hospital early. She opened the *Halifax Herald,* and showed Katie the headline: *War May Be Declared by England Within Twenty-Four Hours.*

"I'm sorry, Gwen," was all Katie could say.

Gwen spent the day baking to help take her mind of the crisis. Katie went to her room and wrote a letter to Ruth and one to Birdie. She had made a promise to write her sister every day and she tried to do this, even if she only wrote her a few lines.

The next day it was confirmed: Britain was at war with Germany. Already, men in khaki uniforms were parading the streets of Halifax. In the newspaper, it was reported that small boats and fishing vessels were to keep within the harbor between sunset and sundown. They were warned if they did not obey, they were liable to be fired at. Katie felt an uneasiness she'd never felt before.

She soon learned though that not everyone shared Gwen's grim view of war. Day and night, people thronged the street, singing, cheering and waving flags. Posters were distributed throughout the city calling for volunteers. From all over Halifax, crowds came to watch the bulletin boards outside the newspaper offices. They were there from early in the morning until late at night.

Gwen read all the newspaper accounts. "They expect the war to last no longer than a few weeks," she told Katie. "Prime Minister Borden says the troops will be home by Christmas."

Will Hannah be home for Christmas? Katie wondered. Already, the summer was almost used up. In less than two weeks, it would be Labour Day. On September 2, classes would begin at the academy. Katie's stomach tightened in dread at the thought of going to a strange school. Even more troubling was the fact that once school started, she would have less time to look for Hannah.

Nearly every day Katie went searching for her sister. Halifax had thousands of families, and it was almost impossible to find someone if you didn't have an address. Since the war, more and more people were crowding into the city, and the streets were becoming more and more crowded. Things were not turning out as Katie had planned. Also, she was having nagging doubts. Would Hannah remember her? She had been with Mrs. Abbott for ten months now. It was likely Hannah thought of her as her mother. She might not remember that she had another family.

Chapter 16

SEPTEMBER 1914

*A*s Katie turned off Spring Garden and onto Brunswick, she recalled Gwen's parting words: *Strangers soon become friends.* Katie silently repeated the words to comfort herself. But as she approached the Halifax Academy, she felt her stomach tighten. What would be expected of her in this new school? Would she be able to keep up with the work? And would the other students want to be friends with her?

The clock on Citadel Hill told her it was twenty minutes past eight. Still forty minutes before classes began. Katie waited in the deserted schoolyard until the doors opened, then went inside to find the main office. The office clerk, a short, plump woman, gave her a form to fill out. Katie filled in her name as Kate Andrews, using the name on her birth certificate. After giving her directions to her classroom, the clerk handed her a list of books she would need for the term. Katie was delighted that *Oliver Twist* and *Little Dorrit* were on the list.

A tall woman with dark hair and dark eyes—Katie assumed she was the teacher—stood at the front of the classroom. Her quick smile put Katie at ease. "You may sit in that seat over there," she said, pointing to an empty desk by the window. The girl in the desk across from it looked as tall and gangly as a boy. Her long legs were twisted around the desk in front of her. In the desk behind her was a girl with reddish brown hair held back in tortoise shell combs. She was wearing a stylish dress with a nipped-in waist.

It was still early, and students were still filing into the classroom. "Over here, Caroline," called the red-haired girl.

Katie felt a pang of loneliness. Back home she knew everyone. She wanted more than anything to be friends with the girls around her, but she was too shy to start a conversation.

"I'm Miss Foster," the teacher announced after everyone was seated. "I want to welcome you back to the academy. I hope you all had a pleasant summer. Before we begin, could you please stand for our anthem?" The students rose then, and began to sing.

Heaven bless the Mayflower
Blooming in the sea
Star of Nova Scotia
Emblem of the free.

Katie didn't know the words, and she felt strangely out of place. Back home, they sang "Ode to Newfoundland" and "God Save the King." But this was Canada, and Newfoundland had very little to do with Canada. Even the money here was different. As Birdie often reminded them, England was their mother country.

When they sat down again, Miss Foster began calling names from the register. "Ruth Allen, John MacDougall, Samuel Bennet, Mary MacDonald . . ." As their names were called, the students raised their hands. Katie tried to remember all their names. The red-haired girl was Helen and the pretty girl with the stylish clothes was Margaret.

"Lucy MacDougall?"

The girl across from Katie raised her hand.

"Will John be coming back this year?"

"No, Miss," Lucy answered. "He's enlisting."

The teacher shook her head, and Katie thought she saw something like sadness in her eyes. She continued to go through the list of students, and when all the names were called, she turned her attention to Katie. "We have a new student with us this year," she said, glancing at Katie's registration form. "Kate Andrews. Welcome."

All heads turned, and she was aware of their eyes on her.

"Kate is from St. Anthony, Newfoundland. The teacher pointed to a tattered map that hung on the wall behind her. "Newfoundland is here. And St. Anthony is up here, right at the very tip of the country. Isn't that right, Miss Andrews?"

"Yes, Miss," Katie, said, shyly. She wasn't used to being the center of attention among so many strangers.

"Your dad must be a fisherman," said the girl with the stylish clothes.

"Papa's dead. He got drowned on the Labrador."

"On the what?"

"The Labrador. We used to go there to fish."

Miss Foster referred to the map again. "Labrador is over here near Quebec," she said. "The country belongs to Newfoundland."

"Isn't it only Eskimos and Indians who live in Labrador?" another boy asked.

Forgetting her shyness, Katie told them of the native population: the hunter Innu, and the inland and coastal Inuit. She told them about the livyers, explaining they were descendants of British servants who came with the fur trading company and had intermarried with the native population.

Miss Foster looked pleased, and she smiled and nodded as Katie spoke.

"It used to be my home every summer until Papa got drowned," she explained. "Mama died that same year, and I went to live in the orphanage at St. Anthony."

"An orphanage?" Margaret gasped. "You're an orphan?"

Katie flushed. She hoped the other students wouldn't pity or scorn her. She couldn't be certain from the faces that stared back at her.

"I come to Canada so that I might finish my education," she announced proudly. "Someday, I will be a nurse."

"Well," said Miss Foster, "we have two other girls here who also want to be nurses. Miss MacDougall, here," she said, gesturing to the girl across from her. "And also Miss White." She nodded toward a girl in the front row.

Both girls turned to give Katie a warm smile, and she relaxed a little.

The morning dragged by slowly. The lessons were different from what she was used to, and Katie worried that she might not be able to keep up with the others.

At noon, the gun on the Citadel went off with a loud bang, startling Katie. Lack of sleep had made her nervous and jumpy. At the sound of the gun, students got out of their seats and began to leave. She followed them out of the classroom and into the schoolyard.

⤺

Katie leafed idly through a small stack of letters the mailman had slipped through the slot in the door. Although she had been in Halifax for nearly three months now, she still marvelled that mail came every day. She felt a surge of pleasure at recognizing Ruth's neat printing. Smiling, she opened the envelope and removed the single sheet of paper. *Katie, I like your stories about Canada. Write and tell me more. I miss you a whole lot. Love, Ruth.* There was another letter from Matt, and she opened it eagerly. *I am sorry that you have not had much luck finding Hannah,* he wrote. *However, I have new information I know will be useful. I went back to the neighborhood where the Abbotts used to live. Mr. Abbott's rightful name is Edward Silas, which would explain why the operator could not find his name. Anyway, I found someone who gave me his address in Halifax.*

Katie felt her heart quicken as she continued to read. *The Abbotts live at 7879 Victoria Drive* . . . Matt had written more, but Katie was already out the door. She knew Victoria Drive was down by the park. Sometimes, when she and Gwen went to the park on Sunday afternoons, they would walk past that street on the way.

Katie ran most of the way. By the time she reached Victoria Drive, she was out of breath. The houses on the street were large, most of them with automobiles in the driveway. Number 7879 stood among acres of trees, and was even bigger than the others. Built of gray brick, it had a turret on one side that made it look like a castle. Katie's heart gave a sudden leap at the sight of a high-wheeled pram that stood on the veranda. Before she could think about what she was going to say, she ran up the marble steps and rang the doorbell. Immediately, she reproached herself for being so impulsive. What could she say to those people? She really should have planned the visit more carefully.

A maid with a white pinafore over a black uniform opened the door. She looked quizzically at Katie. "Can I help you?" she said briskly.

Katie was at a loss for words. "I . . . I'm Kate . . . Kate Andrews," she stammered. "I . . . I came here from Newfoundland . . . from St. Anthony . . . I . . ."

"Oh. Mrs. Borden has been expecting you. Come

in. I'll tell her you're here."

Puzzled, Katie stepped into the large foyer.

"Who is it, Lily?" came a voice from inside. A large woman with a broad face appeared in the foyer. Her greying hair was swept carefully into a knot at the back of her head. Her small black eyes studied Katie with interest.

"It's the girl from St. Anthony."

The woman clasped her hands. "From the head-quarters."

It wasn't a question, but Katie nodded. She was wondering if she was at the right house when she saw the photographs on the wall in front of her—photographs Mr. Abbot had taken during his visit to the Labrador. There was a close-up of Hannah and Mrs. Abbott, the same picture Katie had seen in the newspaper. In other photographs, women and children were spreading fish on flakes. It felt strange seeing people she knew in such an unfamiliar surrounding. There was also a picture of the *Strathcona* with Dr. Grenfell standing on deck. Katie realized this picture must have been taken at another time.

"Daniel said he'd be sending someone from the Grenfell Mission," Mrs. Borden said.

"Daniel?"

The woman looked Katie up and down. "My, but

you are so young," she said. "What is your connection with the mission?"

"I ... uh ... I used to live at Dr. Grenfell's orphanage."

"An orphan? Oh dear. I thought Daniel said it was a nurse he was sending."

It dawned on Katie then that the woman had mistaken her for someone else.

"I ... I'm not ..." Katie tried to explain.

The woman went right on talking as if she hadn't heard her. "Some of my lady friends here in Halifax want to form a Grenfell association. We've been looking for someone from the headquarters to speak to us. But I'm sure Daniel must have explained all that."

Katie knew that Dr. Grenfell's mission had now become the International Grenfell Association. Branches were being set up in Canada and the United States. But as the woman spoke, Katie craned her neck around the doorway, hoping to get a glimpse of Hannah. All she could see was a wide hallway panelled in light oak.

"Oh, and here I am all dressed to go out," the woman continued. "My lady friends are meeting for lunch on Saturday. Could you come at that time?" She spoke with an air of someone who was used to getting what she wanted.

"But ..."

"Oh dear, if I don't hurry, I really will be late."

The woman turned her attention to the maid. "Lily, please take care of our guest. Give her the details of lunch on Saturday."

Before Katie could utter another word, the woman turned and walked away.

Katie turned to the maid who was looking slightly amused. "Who is she?" she half whispered. She realized the woman had not introduced herself.

"That's Fanny Borden, Mrs. Abbott's aunt. She's visiting from Ontario. She's the president of the Grenfell association in Ottawa." She rolled her eyes. "All she ever talks about. Her nephew's been looking for someone from some mission." She peered closely at Katie. "He must have found you at the last minute."

Katie didn't answer. She stared at the pictures on the wall. There was a close-up of Maud Skinner's lined, weather-beaten face. In another photograph, a seagull was pecking at the fish that had been spread out to dry.

"Mr. Abbott took those pictures while he was in Labrador," Lily said. "It was he who got Mrs. Borden interested in the Grenfell mission. He came back with all kinds of stories."

And a baby, Katie thought.

She didn't know how she could help, but she wasn't going to miss an opportunity to see Hannah.

"What time should I be here on Saturday?"

Chapter 17

LUNCH AT THE ABBOTTS'

"Silas Abbott!" Gwen exclaimed. "He is well-known in Halifax, but better known in Newfoundland. They have been connected with the sealing and fishing industry for years."

"Wonder why he got out of it?"

"Most likely, he still owns some of the sealing vessels," Gwen said. "Someone else is probably running the operation for him." She gazed steadily at Katie. "But I don't understand. Why are they inviting you to lunch?"

Katie explained that Fanny Borden and her friends wanted to form a Grenfell Association in Halifax. "They wants to talk to somebody who knows about the mission."

She felt a small prickle of guilt about omitting the fact that she went to the Abbotts' looking for Hannah. It wasn't that she wanted to deceive Gwen. She just wasn't sure how Gwen would feel about her search for Hannah. Would she have invited Katie to Halifax knowing her main motive was to find her sister? Still, she felt bad not being completely honest.

"Miss Storr wrote in her last letter that since the Grenfell mission registered in St. John's, associations are springing up all over the place," Gwen said. "It's good that so many people are taking an interest."

A thought suddenly struck Katie. What if Mrs. Abbott recognized her from that time on the beach? It wasn't likely she would. The beach was crowded, and Katie had stood at a distance. Besides, more than a year had passed since that time. Still, it was one more thing for her to worry about. She should have told Fanny Borden the truth. Papa used to say that if you let someone believe something you know is not true, you are deceiving them. And to deceive someone is the same as lying. She would set it all straight when she was reunited with Hannah, Katie told herself. She often imagined her reunion with her sister. Hannah would come running to her, wrapping her arms around Katie's neck. Anyone seeing them would know they belonged together. Surely, the Abbotts would understand.

"A penny for your thoughts," Gwen said.

Shortly before twelve on Saturday, Katie stood outside the Abbotts' large house. Her hands trembled as she rang the doorbell. She took a deep breath to quell the nervousness in her stomach.

"Kate Andrews?"

"Lucy?" Katie exclaimed. The last person she'd expected to see was Lucy McDougall who sat across from her at the Halifax Academy. "I didn't know yeh worked here."

"Usually only on Thursday afternoon and Sunday," Lucy said, taking Katie's coat. "But Mrs. Abbott called yesterday saying she was entertaining important guests." She gave Katie a look that clearly told her she didn't expect her to be one of them.

Before Katie could explain, Fanny appeared in the doorway. "Oh, there you are, Kate. I'm so happy you could make it, dear. The gals have already arrived, and they are anxious to meet you." She turned to Lucy. "Girl, the water pitcher needs to be filled."

Katie felt light-headed as Mrs. Borden ushered her down a wide marble-tiled hallway into an enormous living room. How would they feel about her when they found out the real reason she was here?

The "gals," three gray-haired women perched on a large sofa, smiled at her when she came into the room. Mrs. Abbot sat across from them on a love seat. Sitting next to her was a thin little man with a short mustache.

Katie's eyes darted around the room searching for Hannah, but she was nowhere to be seen.

The room was elegant with a high ornate ceiling and long narrow windows. Elaborate chairs and sofas in shades of beige and green were grouped around the room. A large stone fireplace stood at one end with a hearth large enough to stand in.

"This is Kate Andrews," Fanny announced. She gestured toward Mrs. Abbott. "This is my niece, Jane Abbott."

Katie saw that she had grown pale and thin since she'd seen her on the landwash in Labrador. "Andrews?" she repeated.

Katie stood rooted to the spot. For sure, Mrs. Abbott would have known Hannah's last name. Why didn't she think of that? Her heart began to beat faster. She wiped her moist palms on the skirt of her dress.

"Where did you come from?" she asked.

"Kate's from the headquarters," Mrs. Borden said. "St. Anthony."

Mrs. Abbott seemed to consider this. "I imagine Andrews is a common name in Newfoundland and Labrador."

"Yes," Katie said. "There are many Scottish descendants."

"You look familiar," Mrs. Abbot replied. "Have you been in Halifax long?"

"Since July. I'm a student at the Halifax Academy."

"Well," Mrs. Borden said. "Let me introduce you to the rest of the folks." She turned to the man sitting next to Mrs. Abbott. "This man, who followed me all the way from Ottawa, is my husband, Clarence Borden." She laughed as if she'd told a joke.

Mr. Borden rose to shake Katie's hand. "Very pleased to meet you," he said in a heavy British accent.

"And these," Aunt Fanny said, gesturing to the three women on the sofa, "are my friends, Ede, Violet and Henny."

The women all wore bright red lipstick and elaborate jewellery. Katie could smell the sickly sweet odor of their perfume. They were dressed as if they were going to a party. Katie was wearing one of her best dresses, but felt shabby beside them.

Shortly, Mrs. Abbott led them through a set of French doors into an impressive dining room. This room was even more elegant than the sitting room. Large, colorful paintings adorned the walls. A long table, that could easily accommodate a dozen people, was laden with fancy china and silverware. There were brass candlestick holders, crystal water glasses and fancy dishes filled with pickles, olives, and mustard. Katie found her silverware next to a white starched linen napkin. She felt like a character in a book. *Good Lord, what have I got myself into now?*

"Everything looks lovely, dear." Violet exclaimed. "Especially that centre piece."

Katie followed her gaze to a large crystal bowl in the centre of the table. It was filled with pink water and had rose petals and lighted candles floating on top.

Mrs. Abbott looked pleased. "Delightful to look at," she agreed.

Katie remembered how she had once used those same words to describe Hannah.

"Mr. Abbott is in Newfoundland," Fanny said to no one in particular. "He'll not be joining us for lunch."

Katie wondered if his visit to Newfoundland had anything to do with the inquiry into the seal hunt disaster last spring. He owned some of the sealing vessels, after all. Matt had written that all St. John's was up in arms. Many felt the men had been sent to their death because of greed. They had demanded an investigation.

"Clarence, would you give the blessing?" Mrs. Abbott asked. She sat at the head of the table, a little silver bell beside her. Whenever she wanted something, she rang, and Lucy came running in from the kitchen.

As Mr. Borden prayed, Katie glanced out the tall windows that were framed with gold velvet curtains and looked out upon green lawns and hedges. A stone birdbath was near the window, and there was a garden with rows of violets, geraniums, and various other flowers Katie couldn't identify. She sat between Ede and Violet, feeling out of place in such posh surroundings. She was so nervous, she could feel her insides quiver. What if she used the wrong spoon or fork?

Lucy made frequent trips to the dining room, refilling water glasses and bringing in large platters of steaming shrimp, rice, and vegetables. Katie pushed the food around on her plate, and every so often was able to choke down a forkful.

All through the meal, her thoughts were on Hannah, and she kept looking toward the door, half expecting her to come toddling into the dining room. Where were they keeping her? At home, she ate all her meals with the family. Katie had not once heard her sister's name mentioned. She should have told them she was Hannah's sister. The longer she put it off, the harder it was going to be. And how would they feel about her, knowing she was there under false pretences?

Aunt Fanny and her friends made small talk all through lunch. Good help was so hard to find. By the time they trained a servant, she was ready to leave and get married. They had to turn around and train someone else. It was better to hire widows; they were less likely to leave. Katie listened, feeling more and more out of place. Perspiration gathered on her forehead, and from time to time, she used her linen napkin to wipe her damp hands.

It wasn't until Lucy brought dessert—a rich looking chocolate cake with fudge icing—that Fanny turned her attention to Katie. "Now then," she said, "tell us all about the headquarters."

Katie's mouth went dry and she reached for a glass of water. She tried to keep the quiver out of her voice as she told them what it was like living at Dr. Grenfell's orphanage. She rephrased some of the things Birdie wrote in her last letter. A new nursing station had opened at Spotted Islands, and a new hospital at North West River. "There's four hospitals and six nursing stations now," she told them.

Fanny nodded her double chins in approval. "Dr. Grenfell must be kept busy every minute."

In Birdie's words, Dr. Grenfell had been too busy making a show of himself to be a proper doctor. Even Gwen felt he enjoyed being a celebrity more than anything else. But Katie knew this wasn't what these ladies wanted to hear. "He's much busier as a fund-raiser and author than as a doctor," she said. "Most of th' work is left to Dr. Mason, who came to St. Anthony from Boston."

"By Jove, sounds like that Grenfell chap is doing a fine job over there," said Mr. Borden who had been silent up until now. "From Britain, you say?"

Violet dabbed at her lips with a linen napkin. "He's done so much for those poor, unfortunate people."

"His work is becoming a movement," exclaimed Henny.

"Tell me about Mrs. Grenfell," Aunt Fanny said eagerly.

"The dear woman has made so many sacrifices," spouted Ede. "Can you imagine leaving the luxury of a beautiful home in Lake Forest to go to some godforsaken place in Newfoundland." She clicked her tongue in sympathy. "I saw a picture in the newspaper of where she's living now. A tiny log hut, not much bigger than our doghouse."

Katie wiped her mouth with a napkin to hide her smile. Gwen had shown her that picture weeks ago in *Among the Deep Sea Fishers,* a magazine put out by the mission. The magazine had got it all wrong. "That log hut is a deer hunter's shelter," Katie explained. "The doctor and Mrs. Grenfell have a beautiful new house in St.

Anthony."

"You mean she doesn't live in a hut?" Ede sounded disappointed. "Well, I'm sure the dear soul must have made some sacrifices."

Katie had lost some of her nervousness and was feeling slightly amused by the four ladies. It made her uncomfortable though, the way the women kept referring to the people of Labrador and Newfoundland as "those poor, unfortunate fisher folks." She knew that most people in Newfoundland considered themselves lucky if they could work. The only poor people were those without limbs or who were too sick to work and had to go on the dole. Her father often reminded them how lucky they were to have a roof over their head and food on the table.

Katie glanced across the table at Mrs. Abbott. Strange, she thought, with all this talk about Newfoundland and Labrador that she never once mentioned having adopted a child from there.

Mr. Borden stifled a yawn. Mrs. Borden rang her little bell, and Lucy came running into the kitchen to take away the dessert dishes.

"Why don't we have our coffee in the living room?" Mrs. Abbott suggested, rising to her feet. "We'll be more comfortable in there."

Lucy came into the living room with a pot of coffee and some cups and saucers on a tray. Katie thought she looked tired, and felt a tinge of guilt having her wait on her.

She had told Fanny and her friends everything she knew about the mission, and now Fanny turned to another topic. "Do you have brothers or sisters, Kate?"

"I have a sister, Ruth, back in St. Anthony." She said nothing about Hannah, but seeing an opportunity to inquire about her, she turned to Jane Abbott. "Do you have children, Mrs Abbott?" She tried to make the question sound casual, but she was aware of the tremor that had crept into her voice.

"She has a little girl," Aunt Fanny answered for her. "Our darling angel, Daisy. "

Daisy. They changed her name. Where is she? Surely I'll get to see her before I leave.

"Where is she?" Aunt Fanny asked as if reading Katie's thoughts. "I haven't seen the little darling since this morning."

Katie held her breath. Her heart began to race.

"She's sleeping. The housekeeper says she's been restless all morning."

"Oh dear, I hope she's not coming down with something," said Fanny.

"I hear there's been an outbreak of chicken pox in the North End," piped up Violet.

"Best to keep her inside and warm," offered Ede.

Fanny turned to Katie. "And who is taking care of your younger sister?"

"She's staying at the children's home."

"Oh, the poor wee thing," clucked Henny. "Alone without her family."

"She's being well taken care of," Katie said quickly, surprised at how defensive she sounded.

Henny gave her a quick look. "Well, I'm sure she is, dear, if she's with the Grenfell mission."

This sent the women off on a tangent about all the good things they could do for the less fortunate once a Grenfell association was established in Halifax.

Lucy came in to collect the china and to see if anything else was needed.

Mr. Borden stretched and yawned. "Well, I'm off," he said.

"And I should to be getting home, too," said Violet. "My daughter is coming this afternoon."

All three ladies stood simultaneously.

"Would you like for us to have the car brought around for you, Kate?" Mrs. Abbott asked.

Katie realized she was being dismissed. She wouldn't be seeing Hannah today. Disappointment hit her like a slammed door. She knew she had to find a way to get back to the Abbotts' to see her sister.

Chapter 18

THE NORTH END

"Oh, dear," Miss Foster said, looking around the classroom at the empty desks. "Such a busy time of year for my students to have come down with chicken pox. I wanted to get started on Charles Dickens, and there's the term essay I wanted to talk about."

Katie glanced at the empty desk across the aisle. She'd been hoping to have a word with Lucy, to find out anything she could about Hannah. Apparently Lucy had come down with chicken pox too.

Katie was beginning to feel she would never see her sister again. On Sunday, she had hung around outside the Abbotts' house, hoping someone would bring Hannah outside, but except for the servants no one left. At times, she thought she should march inside the Abbotts' house and set them straight, demand they give Hannah back to her. But she knew she needed a plan.

During the next couple of days, more students came down with chicken pox. Miss Foster grew frantic. "If this keeps up, we will have to close our school." She looked around the classroom. "How many of you have had chicken pox?"

Katie's arm shot up along with a number of others.

"I'm going to need volunteers," the teacher continued. "I need students to deliver papers and homework to those who are out sick. Only those of you who have been infected, of course. Keep your hands up please, so I can see who you are."

She walked briskly up and down the aisles, handing out papers. "Thomas, can you take John Wilson's? And Rachel, I'm going to give you Susan Cain's. And Kate . . . let me see now—"

"I can take Lucy's, if you like," Katie said quickly. "Lucy MacDougall's."

"Thank-you, Kate." Miss Foster rifled through the heap of papers until she found Lucy's. She put the paper on Katie's desk, and moved on to the next student.

Katie looked down at the paper that had Lucy's name and address written in the top right-hand corner. She lived at 3946 Gottingen Street.

When Miss Foster finished handing out the papers, she went back to her desk and opened her copy of

Oliver Twist. "Class, please turn to page thirty-two of your text," she said.

There was a shuffling of books, and pages were being turned nosily.

"Dickens was a great author," the teacher continued, "and a remarkable man. But to understand his work, it is important to know something of his experiences." She looked around the classroom. "Do any of you know anything about Dickens' background?"

Katie remembered that Gwen's grandfather had once met Mr. Dickens in England. She told Katie that he once lived in the poor house. She raised her hand.

"Yes, Kate."

"Mr. Dickens was poor."

"Yes. That's true. And because he had experienced poverty himself, he had sympathy for the oppressed and the downtrodden." The teacher began pacing the aisle. "You must understand that the England of seventy-five years ago was divided by a rigid class structure. There was a great gulf between the upper and lower classes. Women and children sometimes worked fourteen hours a day in factories." She paused as if gathering her thoughts. "It was a world of slums and poverty, a world where boys and girls had very little chance to get an education."

Katie thought of the children on the Labrador working from dawn to dusk. There were many like Etta who had never learned to read or write. In Fathom Harbour, boys as young as nine and ten years old sometimes went fishing with their fathers.

"Dickens was only twelve when he went to work in a blackening factory," Miss Foster continued. "His job was to cover and label the pots of blackening. He desperately wanted to escape from this drudgery and go to school. He wanted to grow up to be a learned man."

Katie listened with interest, knowing exactly how the young Dickens must have felt. She couldn't help but feel a surge of gratitude. She would be fifteen years old next month, but instead of the drudgery of going out to service as Etta was mostly likely doing now, she had the privilege of being able to attend a good school.

As soon as school was out, she headed toward the North End to find Lucy's house. Katie was beginning to grow familiar with the streets now and felt more comfortable when she had to go somewhere. At the end of Brunswick Street, she turned onto Gottingen, and after she had walked only a few blocks, the pavement ended. The streets became more narrow, the sharp odor of wood smoke stronger. The houses here did not have the elaborate trim or ornate frills of the houses in the South End. She passed small factories, shops, restaurants, and Chinese laundries. She walked past a church, its crumbling bricks black with coal soot. After a while, she found herself in a neighbor-hood of small rundown houses. A wooden cart rattled by, drawn by two horses. It splashed dirty water from a big pothole on her cotton stockings. A few children in shabby clothes were playing in the street, and they stared warily at Katie.

After some time, she found the address she was looking for: one of a row of houses huddled together. Katie walked up the dusty path to the door where a sign warned in red letters: *We Are In Quarantine.* Ignoring the sign, she knocked on the door.

The tall, thin woman who greeted her had the same color eyes as Lucy. She glanced anxiously at the sign, and then at Katie.

She quickly explained why she had come. "I've already had the chicken pox," she added.

Mrs. MacDougall's face relaxed. "Come in," she said kindly, holding the door open.

Katie walked through a small porch and into the kitchen. A big iron stove dominated the room, and on the floor beside it was a bucket of coal. The walls were white, flaking in places, exposing the blue paint that had been there before. A washstand in the corner held a porcelain picture and basin. The only pictures on the wall were a portrait of King George V and a calendar compliments of *Hills & Son Ltd. 3062 Hollis Street.* The room reminded Katie of their own kitchen back in Fathom Harbour, and somehow she found this strangely comforting.

"I'm Meg McDougall, Lucy's mother. It was kind of you to bring Lucy's schoolwork."

Kate remembered the real reason for her visit, and felt a tinge of shame. "Lucy will be pleased to have company," Mrs. McDougall said. "Her brothers and sisters have been sent off to relatives. For the past couple of days, the poor girl's been bored to tears."

She led Katie down a cramped hallway where the floorboards creaked under their weight. She opened the door to a small room where Lucy was propped up on pillows in an iron bed, reading. There were pox marks on her face, and her dark hair hung as limp as cooked spinach. Her eyes widened with surprise when she saw Katie.

"Kate was kind enough to bring your schoolwork," Mrs. McDougall explained. She smiled at Katie. "Can I get you anything? Cake? Tea?"

"No, thanks," Katie told her.

"Well, if you need anything, I'll be in the kitchen," she said kindly, then closed the door.

Once Kate was alone with Lucy, she felt suddenly shy. "I . . . I brought your homework," she said unnecessarily.

"Thank-you," Lucy replied, almost too politely.

For a while, they talked about school, the conversation stiff and formal. Katie, remembering that Lucy wanted to be a nurse, told her about meeting the matron at the Victoria General Hospital. "We expect high standards from our student trainees." Katie mimicked the matron's voice exactly.

Lucy laughed. "I hear she's a real sourpuss. Maybe by the time we get there, she'll be retired." The ice was broken, and both girls became more relaxed. Lucy told Katie that her mother thought the Halifax Academy was such a good school that she wanted Lucy to go even if it meant walking a great distance every day. Lucy's younger brothers and sisters went to Richmond. Her brother, John, had attended the academy until he enlisted in the army.

"I plan to work a year after I finish school," Lucy said. "I need to save money."

"Will yeh keep working for the Abbotts?" Katie asked, finding a way to bring the subject around to Hannah.

"They pay well," Lucy told her. "But I would rather work in a store or a restaurant. I don't mind taking care of their little girl, but I hate housework."

"What's she like?"

"Mrs. Abbott? She can be quite demanding."

"I meant the baby," Katie said with a catch in her voice.

"Daisy? She's a good baby. She's already starting to talk."

Of course, she'd be talking. She was already talking when the Abbotts took her away.

"Is she a happy baby?"

Lucy gave her an odd look. "She seems to be. But of course, I'm only with her on Thursday afternoons. I usually take her for a walk while Mrs. Abbott plays bridge with her friends."

For a moment, Katie considered telling Lucy that Hannah was her sister. Maybe Lucy could help her. "Where do you take Daisy for walks?" she asked.

"Usually to the Public Gardens if the weather is good. She loves feeding the ducks and swans."

Katie wanted to know more, but at that moment Mrs. McDougall poked her head around the door. "We will be having supper in about an hour," she said. "You are welcome to stay, Kate."

"Thank-you." Katie said, "but I got to get home." She remembered then that she had promised Gwen that she would cut up vegetables for a stew.

By the time Katie left Lucy's house, the shadows of evening were already starting to gather. As she strolled along the darkening streets, a plan took shape in her mind. As soon as school was out on Thursday, she would go to the Public Gardens. She would "run into" Lucy who would be taking Hannah for a walk.

I'll see Hannah on Thursday, Katie told herself as she hurried home, her heart thumping with anticipation.

Chapter 19

"WHERES MY SISTER ?"

"*D*aisy had the chicken pox, but she's feeling much better now," Lucy informed Katie. "I was talking to Mrs. Abbott yesterday and she wants me to come by on Thursday."

It was Lucy's first day back to school after being away for more than a week, and they were eating their lunch on the slope of Citadel Hill. Lucy still had traces of pox marks on her face, and Katie thought she looked pale and tired.

She had been hanging around the Abbotts' house all week, sometimes watching for hours. People came and went, but she had not seen Hannah. Once, Katie had even gone to the door with the pretence of wanting Aunt Fanny's address in Ottawa, telling the maid she had new information on the Grenfell Mission. The maid had Katie wait in the foyer while she got the address from Jane Abbott.

"The Abbotts are going to England to visit Mr. Abbott's mother," Lucy said, interrupting Katie's thoughts.

Katie's head jerked up. "When?"

"They're leaving at the end of the week."

Katie felt her heart sink. She couldn't let them take Hannah away. And besides, traveling during wartime was dangerous. "When are they coming back?"

"It could be months," Lucy said. She laughed at Katie's stricken look. "It's okay, really. I can always get a job babysitting the neighbor's kids until they return."

Kate sat in stunned silence.

Lucy stood up. "We should get back," she said, brushing breadcrumbs from her dress. "The bell will ring any minute now."

For the next couple of days, Katie felt as restless as a crow in a cage. It rained on Tuesday and again on Wednesday, and the forecast called for rain on Thursday. She knew Lucy wouldn't take Hannah outside if it rained.

Relief filled Katie when she awoke on Thursday morning to see that the sun was already breaking through the clouds. She could hardly concentrate on her schoolwork, and made so many mistakes in math that Miss Foster told her she would have to take the math problems home and work on them there. By the time the bell rang, every nerve in Katie's body was like a string on a violin that had been wound too tight.

She walked briskly up Spring Garden Road and pushed open the wrought iron gate, her heart hammering. She sat on a wooden bench and stared out at the pond. After only a few minutes, she felt restless, and got up and paced a narrow gravel path that wound through the garden. The leaves on the trees had changed color, and many had fallen to the ground. Kate walked over to the gazebo and sat down on the edge of the wooden platform. After only a few minutes, she got up and began pacing idly. A thought struck her: what if Lucy had changed her mind? What if she took Hannah for a walk in Point Pleasant Park instead? Should she go to the Abbotts'? What if Lucy had already left? Katie stood up, torn by indecision. If Lucy took Hannah to the park, Katie wouldn't get to see her today.

She left the Public Gardens, and ran all the way to the South End. By the time she reached Victoria Drive, she was gasping for breath. Hiding behind a large oak, she waited for Lucy to bring Hannah outside. She watched as a woman came out of the house, and minutes later, a man rang the doorbell. She waited fifteen minutes, but there was no sign of Lucy. What if Lucy had left already? She would just have to wait until she came back.

Five minutes later, Lucy appeared on the veranda with a bundle in her arms. Katie watched as she put Hannah in her pram and tucked a blanket around her. Not able to stand it any longer, Kate stepped out from behind the tree and waved.

Lucy didn't wave back. To Katie's dismay, Lucy frowned when she approached her.

Katie felt a sinking feeling in the pit of her stomach.

"Hello, Lucy," she said, her voice trembling.

"What is it you want, Kate?" Lucy's voice was cold.

"Lucy, is something wrong?"

Lucy kept walking, her back stiff. Katie followed her. "Lucy, please don't walk away from me," she pleaded.

Lucy turned to give her a hard, accusing look. "What do you want? Why do you keep hanging around here?"

Hanging around? Katie knew she'd been found out. Fear prickled beneath her skin.

"The servants have seen you," Lucy continued. "And if you don't stop, I'll have to speak with Mrs. Abbott." She turned away from Katie and continued pushing the pram.

Katie stepped in front of her. She had to see Hannah. She couldn't wait another minute. "I just want to see the baby."

Lucy stepped back, a startled look on her face.

With trembling hands, Katie pulled the blankets away from the sleeping child. Gazing down at her, she drew in her breath sharply. The baby looked to be a little more than a year old. A beautiful baby with dark hair and long, thick lashes.

She felt a chill sweep up her spine. "That's not Hannah," she cried out. A dark cloud blotted out the sun. The baby awoke and began to cry.

"Where's my sister? Where's Hannah?" Katie fought to keep the panic out of her voice.

Lucy hovered protectively over the crying child, looking scared.

Filled with anguish, Kate ran up to the Abbotts' door.

A few minutes passed before a large woman wearing a white apron opened the door. It was Mrs. Stoddard, the cook. Katie had met her briefly during her visit to the Abbotts.

"What's the matter, child?" she asked in a calm voice.

All her pent-up frustration came pouring out. She began to cry. "I'm looking for my sister. I'm looking for Hannah."

Mrs. Stoddard took her firmly by the elbow and pulled her inside. "You'll wake Mrs. Abbott," she cautioned. "The poor woman has another one of her headaches. She had to cancel her bridge club this afternoon." She guided Katie down a wide hallway and into a large kitchen. "Sit," she ordered, and Katie sat down at a long wooden table. Pots and pans hung on the wall, along with a long-handled iron skillet. A maid in a pale blue uniform stood at the sink peeling potatoes.

Katie continued to cry.

Without a word, Mrs. Stoddart poured her a cup of strong tea. "Drink," she commanded. "It will calm you."

"Do . . . do . . . you know where Hannah . . . where my sister is?" Katie asked between sobs.

The cook was silent. The maid stopped peeling, knife poised. Katie waited for an answer.

"She's not with us anymore," Mrs. Stoddart said after a few moments.

"She's not . . . not . . . " Oh, dear God. Katie couldn't say the word.

"Oh, no, no." Mrs. Stoddard said hurriedly. "Your sister's fine . . . well as far as I know. It's just that . . . well, Mrs. Abbott felt she couldn't keep her anymore. The child was constantly crying—crying for her *Kay-*

ee." Her dark eyes were so full of compassion that Katie broke into fresh tears.

"It must have been quite distressing for the poor child to be separated from her family." Mrs. Stoddart continued on. "She took to one of the servants here—Rose, I think her name was—as if she was her own mother."

"They've exchanged Hannah for another child?" Katie asked, outraged.

Mrs. Stoddart was thoughtful, and it was as if she was searching for the right words. "It wasn't quite like that, dear." She lowered her voice. "The missus is not what one would call the maternal type, but she really tried with Hannah. It's just that Hannah did not fit into the family. Of course, I have only been here a short time, but I know that when young Rose left, Mrs. Abbott was at her wit's end. When Rose came back for visits, Hannah would cry for her. Rose often took the little one on overnight visits." Mrs. Stoddard wiped her hands on her apron. "It got so she was spending more time at Rose's house than here with the Abbotts'. After a time, it was decided that your sister should go live with her."

"And where's she to now, this Rose?"

"Perhaps Mabel would know that." Mrs. Stoddart looked at the maid who had resumed peeling potatoes. "Mabel, you must remember Rose who used to work here?"

"Rose Johnson?"

"Was that her name? Do you happen to know where she is now, Mabel?"

The maid shook her head. "No one's heard from her since she left. Not even the missus."

Chapter 20

NOVEMBER 1914

"No child fitting that description has been left here." Sister Alexa looked dwarfed sitting behind a large mahogany desk.

Katie glanced anxiously at Gwen.

Sister folded her arms inside her habit and peered at them, her eyes blinking rapidly under her round glasses. She reminded Katie of a black and white owl. "Have you tried the Protestant orphanage?"

"We were there yesterday." Katie said, recalling how she and Gwen had looked at rows of cribs filled with babies and toddlers. In the past couple of days, they had searched everywhere. Gwen had contacted the police and had even put Hannah's picture in the newspaper. She had tried to contact Mrs. Abbott, but they had already left for England. The servants didn't know when they would return.

The nun made a gesture of helplessness. "It's a sad story," she said. "The only thing we can do now is pray for the little one." She let her eyes stray to the photograph of Hannah and the piece of paper with Gwen's address and phone number. "And of course I will contact you if the child is brought to us."

Gwen thanked Sister Alexa for her time, and she and Katie left the orphanage.

"I know you must be disappointed, Katie," Gwen said as they started down Quinpool Road.

"Thank you, Gwen," Katie said, quietly. She wondered now why she felt she had to keep her search for Hannah a secret.

Gwen had been very understanding. "I never thought it right that you should be separated from your sister," she said, after Katie had explained everything.

"I'll get her back," Katie had said her voice full of determination. "She belongs with me."

"Of course," Gwen had agreed. "And I will do everything I can to help you find her."

Gwen rested her hand on Katie's shoulder, jolting her out of her thoughts. "I have to go to work now. Are you going be okay?"

Katie nodded. It was Saturday and she was out of school. "I really should get my Christmas shopping finished," she said. What she really wanted to do was to go home, go quietly to her bedroom, put her head on her pillow, and cry. But she knew she had to carry on if she was to find Hannah. And she had to get Ruth's gift in the mail in time for Christmas.

"I know only too well what the mail system is like in northern Newfoundland this time of year," Gwen said. "The sooner the parcel is in the mail, the better."

"Yes," Katie agreed. She had already bought Miss Storr's gift. And last week she had picked up a bucket of candy for the children.

They had come to the corner of Jubilee and Robie Street, a location known as Camphill.

"Have fun shopping," Gwen said as they parted company.

"I'll see you this evening," Katie said as she started toward Barrington. The days were getting colder now. Frost coated the ground and the roofs of houses and puddles were hardened into gray ice.

As Katie approached the downtown area, she could hear singing, shouting, and cheering. The waterfront was dotted with people, and it seemed as if the whole city had come downtown to celebrate. A small brass band was playing and there was a carnival-like atmosphere, the mood like that of a public holiday. Katie knew that the enlistment rate in Halifax was one of

the highest in Canada, and whenever a Blue Nose reg-
iment departed, crowds like this showed up to celebrate. Some of the boys at the Halifax Academy had
walked out of school to join the war. Many of them
were afraid the war would be over before they had a
chance to join. Some had already come back wounded; one boy had been killed.

Despite everything, Katie felt her spirits lift as she
walked down Barrington Street. It was only six weeks
before Christmas, and elegant decorations graced the
store windows. Holly and mistletoe hung in doorways,
and Christmas music drifted out onto the sidewalk.
Stores advertised dolls, skates, spinning tops, hats, and
sweaters. She spent the morning and part of the afternoon going in and out of stores, allowing three dollars
out of the money she had so carefully saved. Except
for the small sum she paid Gwen for her board, Katie
had barely touched the money.

At Eaton's she found just the right scarf for Birdie.
For Ruth, Katie bought *Anne of Green Gables,* that
book everyone was raving about. Ruth liked to read,
and Birdie had written that she spent a lot of time in
the library. Katie walked home feeling she had accom-
plished much.

As soon as she walked through the door, she could
tell from the look on Gwen's face that something was

wrong. She took Katie's packages, and pulled out a chair for her to sit down. "What is it?" she asked anxiously.

"It's bad news, Katie," Gwen said, trying to soften the impact.

Katie braced herself, a hundred scenarios dancing in her head. Did something happen to Ruth? Hannah? Her heart was racing.

"It's your aunt," Gwen said.

"Aunt Til?"

"She passed away." Gwen held up an envelope. "This was sent by her neighbor, Mr. Pilgrim. He says she died peacefully in her sleep. I'm very sorry, Katie."

Katie knew her aunt had not been well for some time now, and she was not entirely surprised by the news. Yet sadness overtook her and tears flowed freely. She had hoped to see Aunt Til again before she passed on.

"She was nearly eighty," Gwen said gently. "And she died peacefully, the letter says." She gestured toward the dining room table. "There's a parcel too. Her personal things." She peered intently at Katie, her voice filled with concern. "Are you going to be all right?"

"I'm okay," Katie said. "But I'm goin' to my room now."

"Yes. Of course," Gwen said. "If you need anything, let me know."

Katie picked up the parcel and went into the bedroom, closing the door behind her. She didn't even come out for supper. Her face felt stiff from crying.

It was starting to get dark by the time she opened the box; she had put it off, knowing it would create a fresh wave of pain. There were framed photographs wrapped in newspaper, one of Aunt Til in her nurse's uniform. There was another of Katie's mother and father, taken the year before they died. Sadness pierced Katie's heart, seeing them together in the picture.

Wrapped in layers of tissue paper was Aunt Til's nurse's hat. Katie took it out of the plastic and ran her hand over its smoothness. At the bottom of the box, she found a letter. The single word, *Katie,* was scrawled on the envelope in her aunt's spidery handwriting. Katie picked it up, almost afraid to open it. Slowly, she broke the seal and, with trembling hands, removed the letter. It was dated June 3, 1914, nearly six months ago. Why would Aunt Til write her a letter and not send it?

> *Dearest Katie,*
> *By the time you get to read this letter, I will be gone. I hope it will be a long time from now, but I am getting on in years, and my health is not what it once was. The little house and the land I live on*

*is not worth much, but the Pilgrims next door
have been wanting to buy it. I have arranged that
in the event of my death, Mr. Pilgrim will buy the
house and the money will go to you. It will help
with your nursing training, and help you take
care of the girls.*

*I know how much you want to be a nurse,
Katie, and I have great faith that you will. I also
know how much you want to find Hannah, so
that you can be a family again. And God willing,
you will be all together again.*

Love,
Aunt Til

Katie stayed home from school on Monday morning, but returned in the afternoon, arriving just as the bell was ringing. Most of the students were already seated when she walked into the classroom. Then Lucy was bending over Katie's desk. She was so close, Katie could smell the fragrance of soap on her clothing. "Meet me after school," she whispered.

Before Katie could say anything, Lucy went back to her desk.

Katie found it hard to concentrate on her schoolwork. What did Lucy want to tell her? Katie had done her best to avoid Lucy after the incident at the

Abbotts'. Did she have news about Hannah? It was unlikely since she didn't work for them anymore.

It seemed as if the afternoon would go on forever. Miss Foster continued her lesson on Charles Dickens, and how he lashed out at poverty and injustice. "*Oliver Twist* is a novel about exploitation."

Katie was only half listening. Her thoughts were on Hannah. She was no closer to getting her back than the day she arrived in Halifax. She didn't even know where she was anymore. At least, *Oliver Twist* had a happy ending. Little Oliver fell in with bad company, but was rescued by his half sister, Rose Maylie. In stories, problems always get worked out and people go on to live happily ever after. If only life could be like that.

"Although Fagin and Mrs. Corney are portrayed as vile and despicable characters, they are not the true villains in this novel," Miss Foster continued. "Dickens felt that the true villain was the system that allowed such deplorable acts and even encouraged such evil."

Dr. Grenfell called the truck system evil. He thought it dragged down both fishermen and merchants. A fisherman was once sent to jail because he lied about the amount of fish he'd caught. It had been a bad season, and he didn't think he had enough food to last his family through the winter months.

After school, Katie waited for Lucy in the school-yard. She was smiling as she approached Katie. "How are you, Kate?" she asked softly. "Mrs. Stoddard told me everything."

Katie shrugged. The last thing she wanted was Lucy's pity.

"I talked with Josie Peters too," Lucy continued. "Mrs. Abbott's former servant. She gave me an address where we might find Rose Johnson."

Katie looked at her hopefully.

"It's down on Hollis Street," Lucy said, taking a slip of paper from her book bag. "Number 26. If you like, I can go with you now."

Katie knew Hollis Street was down by the water-front, not far from the academy.

"Why are you doing this, Lucy?"

"I have a little sister of my own," Lucy told her. "If anything happened to Gertie . . . I . . . I will . . . I don't know what I'd do."

"Thanks," Katie whispered. She hugged her friend.

"Let's hope she's still at this address," Lucy said, as they turned off Brunswick onto Argyle and walked toward the harbor with its rows of decaying buildings. On George Street, a scrawny dog followed them, snarling and snapping at their heels.

Many of the buildings had their street numbers missing, and it took them a while before they found number twenty-six, a large, rambling two-story with peeling paint. "Looks like a rooming house," Lucy said as they carefully stepped around garbage that had been spilled on the sidewalk. They walked up a rickety set of steps to the front door.

The rank aroma of stale cooked food, dirty laundry and garbage clogged Katie's nostrils as they stepped into a narrow, dimly lit hallway. Upstairs a door slammed, and at the far end of the hall a loud argument was in progress. A man in a tattered coat sat on the sagging stairs, drinking from a bottle.

"Mother would have a fit if she knew I came here," Lucy said, looking around her.

Katie felt a chill. Little Hannah might be living here. How could Mrs. Abbott have so thoughtlessly given her away?

"It's room number thirteen," Lucy said, looking at the paper in her hand. The hallway was so dark, they could barely make out the room numbers.

Number thirteen was at the back of the house. The door was slightly ajar. Katie knocked, and when there was no answer she knocked again. There was still no answer, and she pushed the room door open a bit further and peeked in. They could see a woman lying face down on a narrow bed, her arms and legs dangling lifelessly over the sides. She looked as if she had been flung there. Katie shot Lucy a worried look. They approached the bed cautiously. The stench of the room was overpowering. Katie felt as if she was going to gag.

The woman on the bed moaned softly, and for a brief moment her eyes fluttered open. At least she's alive, Katie thought. She studied the woman's pale face. The dark hollows around her eyes were like bruises, and her brown hair was matted and tangled.

Katie looked around the room, taking in the mildew that clung to the faded wallpaper. The curtainless window was coated with dirt and grime. A narrow alleyway below the window was littered with paper cartons, tin cans, beer bottles, and old rags. A skinny cat with an ear missing sniffed at the garbage on the ground.

Katie bent down so that her face was close to the woman's. A foul smell crawled up her nostrils. "Rose?"

"Looks like she's passed out," Lucy said. Her eyes strayed to the glint of vodka bottles lined against the wall. "I'll go see if I can find a landlord or someone who might be in charge of the place."

Lucy left and Katie began to shake the woman, gently at first, then more vigorously. It was useless. She lay as still as a corpse. Katie noticed a sink in the corner of the room. Maybe if she washed the woman's face with cold water, it might help bring her around. She looked around for a washrag. The small bureau beside the bed was cluttered with dirty dishes. A nylon stocking was flung over an open box of cereal. At first, she didn't notice the baby doll tossed carelessly on the bureau, its face chipped and one of its porcelain legs broken. Katie's stomach lurched painfully.

Lucy came back in a little while, followed by a short woman dressed in black. "This is Belle, the landlady," she announced.

The woman pursed her lips, making no attempt to hide her disgust at the sight of Rose sprawled on the bed. "You relations of hers?"

"Oh no." Lucy said. "We're just . . . just visiting."

"Owes me two months rent, that one. I warned her I was gonna put her out. Shoulda stuck to me word. Hundreds of people lookin' for rooms since the war started. If I kicked her out tonight, I could have someone in here tomorrow just like that." She flicked her fat fingers.

"Did she have a child with her when she moved in?" Lucy interrupted.

"Not unless she was hiding it in her suitcase." Belle folded her arms over her chest. "Better not be bringin' no brats around here. I tell them when they move in, no youngsters. A girl on the second floor got herself in the family way, and I turned her out." She laughed harshly. "This one here with a child? Ha! She can't even look after her own self."

"We're lookin' for a little girl," Katie explained, a cold hard knot forming in her stomach.

"What would she be doing here?"

"Well, 'tis a long story," Katie said. "But the last we heard, Rose had her."

"Well, she didn't have no youngster when she moved in."

Katie shot Lucy an anxious look. What could Rose have done with Hannah?

At that moment, the woman on the bed began to tremble violently. Her eyes opened and rolled back in her head. "What's wrong with her?" Lucy asked, alarmed.

"She's having DTs," Belle announced, without sympathy. "Just like me late husband." She put her hands on her hips, her mouth grim. "Dear Lord, will I ever be free from drunks?"

Lucy ran out into the hallway. "Call an ambulance," she called.

"Nobody here got a phone but me," the landlady said grumpily. She walked out of the room, taking her time.

Twenty-minutes later, a horse-drawn ambulance pulled up to the door, and two attendants with a stretcher came down the hallway.

Katie felt Lucy's arm on her shoulder. There was nothing for them to do but go home.

Chapter 21

APRIL 1915

"I'm meeting Lucy for coffee and dessert at the Carona café," Katie told Gwen.

"Umm hmm," Gwen muttered, and Katie wondered if she'd even heard her. For the past couple of months, Gwen had seemed preoccupied. Every day, she looked eagerly through the mail as if she was expecting something important. Most of the time, she seemed distracted. Katie often had to repeat herself when she spoke to her. She worried that something serious was happening to Gwen.

By the time she reached Barrington Street, it was already starting to get dark. The Citadel and the buildings of the downtown area were fading into shadows. The streets and sidewalks were alive with soldiers, marines and civilians, all laughing and singing as they strolled along. Katie recalled Miss Foster telling them that since the war began, Halifax had become one of the most important ports in Canada. A large number of soldiers were posted here to protect the city in the event of an enemy attack. Now, as Katie watched them being rowdy and drunk and silly, she wondered how they could protect anyone. She knew they paraded the streets at all hours and that their rowdiness went on long into the night. She glanced at her watch and quickened her pace. Lucy was already at the café, and Katie didn't want to keep her waiting.

A long line of people stood outside the restaurant waiting to be seated. Katie waited in line for everything now, it seemed. Everywhere she went there were long lines of people. As the city became more crowded, the lines became longer. How wrong she had been to think that the war in Europe would not have an effect on her own life. Since the war began, she had seen drastic changes in Halifax. It was having a major effect on the people in Newfoundland and Labrador too. Miss Storr had written that men from all over Newfoundland and Labrador were volunteering to go overseas. Dr. Grenfell had plans to join the Royal Army Medical Corps. Even Miss Storr was talking about joining the armed forces. There was very little fish and what there was could only be sold at the lowest price. Merchants were not sure whether they would be able to collect the cost. Everything had risen in price, and people had been without butter and sugar for weeks. Poachers had killed a number of the reindeer. *They cannot be blamed*, Miss Storr had written. *When families are hungry, men will do whatever they can to provide food for them.*

Katie found Lucy sitting at a small table near the window. "Sorry to take so long," she said, as she slid into a chair across from her.

"I've already placed our orders." Lucy said. "I know how much you love the Carona's mincemeat pie."

"Thanks," Katie said, looking around her. The tables were all filled, as were the stools around the counter. The window was covered with a heavy blackout curtain, making it impossible to see outside. Katie knew there was a large fine for anyone who didn't conceal their lights.

"We got a letter from John today," Lucy said, leaning forward. Voices around them had risen to compete with rattling pots and the clinking of glasses and dinnerware. "He tried to pretend everything's fine, but I know it just isn't true. Kevin Grant, who came home wounded, told me about the bullets that continually crash over the soldiers' heads. He told me about the rats that crawl over soldiers while they sleep." Lucy shuddered. "It's all so horrible and I'm so worried about our John."

Katie touched Lucy's arm. "The war can't last forever," she said. "It's already gone on longer than anyone expected."

"That's what everyone says. But I want John home now."

Katie wanted to tell her that everything was going to be all right, that John would come home. But she didn't know if this was true. "We just have to hope for the best," she said.

The waitress brought their order, and for a little while they ate in silence.

"I haven't had a chance to talk with you since the Easter holidays, Kate," Lucy said, after a while. "Have you had any news at all?"

Katie knew she meant news about Hannah, and a large hole opened up inside her. The pie suddenly felt too thick to go down her throat. She took a sip from her coffee mug. "Nothing." she said, shaking her head.

"I'm sorry, Kate" Lucy said. "I know it must be hard."

"Yes," was all Katie could manage. Months had passed since they had visited Rose Johnson at her rooming house on Hollis Street. Because Gwen worked at the hospital, she was able to get inside information about Rose's condition. She couldn't talk and didn't recognize people. Gwen felt it would take months for Rose to recover. Her parents had come down from New Brunswick to sign a paper to have her put in The Mental. Gwen had questioned them, but they knew nothing about their daughter adopting a baby. Katie knew that Hannah could be anywhere.

Since that horrible day, Katie had thrown herself into her schoolwork. It was the only way she knew how to cope. She prayed that wherever Hannah was, there would be people to love her. But sometimes at night, Katie lay awake, ugly thoughts creeping into her mind.

They were halfway through dessert when two soldiers come into the café. One had thick dark hair and a thin mustache. He looked around the restaurant before choosing a booth. Katie stopped eating, fork poised in midair.

"What is it, Kate? " Lucy asked, following her gaze.

"That soldier over there. He reminds me of somebody."

"For heaven's sake, Kate! All you can see is his uniform. They all look alike in uniform."

"But he reminds me of somebody," she insisted.

A couple of minutes later, the soldier looked directly at Katie. She quickly turned her head, embarrassed to be caught staring.

The soldier got up from his booth and began making his way to her table.

"It's him," Katie whispered to Lucy. She clutched her linen napkin, her heart hammering.

"Katie?" He stood before her now, so tall Katie had to tilt her head back. "Gwen told me I could find you here," he said.

"Matt? . . . I . . . didn't know you'd enlisted."

"I sent a letter from Labrador," he said. "I guess it didn't reach you in time. I'm glad I have this chance to see yeh before I sails for France in the morning."

Katie turned to Lucy who was looking slightly amused. "This is my friend, Lucy McDougall."

"Pleased to meet you," Lucy said, reaching for his hand.

"Why don't yeh come and join us for coffee," he said. "Me and George, a buddy of mine from Bishop Field College, is trying to kill some time before we goes back to our barracks."

Minutes later, they were all squeezed into the small booth, drinking coffee, talking and laughing as if they'd known one another forever.

"Except for the tarpaper roof, our barracks reminds me of a Labrador tilt," Matt told them.

"So you and Kate grew up in the same town?" Lucy said.

"It was really an outport," Matt explained. "I left

there when I was thirteen." He glanced sideways at Katie. "Did Katie ever mention how good she is at handling a dog team?"

"Handling a dog team?" Lucy looked confused.

"Papa kept dogs for hunting and for hauling wood," Katie explained.

"Put all of us fellers to shame," Matt said. "We only wished we was half as good." He glanced at his watch. "Why don't we all go outside for some fresh air?"

"Good idea," Lucy said, buttoning up her sweater. Matt signalled for the waitress.

It was a beautiful night with a full moon shining on the water. On Barrington Street, they passed a group of sailors, their drunken hoots echoing in the calmness. From where they stood, Katie could see a ferry gliding across the water to Dartmouth. Before the war, she remembered how the lights from vessels, freighters, and other ships reflected starkly on the black water. Since the war, ships mostly remained blacked out.

Matt and Katie stopped under a flagpole where the Union Jack was snapping in the night breeze. They could hear George and Lucy laughing in front of them. Katie told Matt about her endless search for Hannah, her voice breaking when she told him about going to Rose Johnson's rooming house.

"I'm sorry, Katie," he said. "I knows how much she

means to you."

"It's hard to be away from Ruth, too," she said. "Although Birdie tells me she's doing well."

"You've been through a lot," Matt said. "I know what it's like to lose both parents. And things are more complicated for you, having the responsibility of two little girls." He took a small deerskin pouch from his jacket pocket. "I brought you somet'ing," he said. He opened the bag and took out a miniature ivory carving.

In the yellow light from the street lamp, Katie saw it was a carving of a Labrador Savannah sparrow. There was so much detail that even from the muted light of the street lamp, Katie could make out the short, notched tail and the line over the eye.

"It's a great work of art," she said. Overcome by Matt's thoughtfulness, she threw her arms around his neck. Startled by her actions, she pulled quickly away.

Matt pulled her against his chest. The top of her head came up just under his chin. She leaned against him, liking the feel of his body against hers. He smelled faintly of soap and pipe tobacco. Katie could feel his even breathing, could hear the faint, steady beat of his heart under the rough material of his uniform.

"Thank-you for the gift," she whispered.

Matt held her at arm's length. "As soon as I seen it, I thought of you, Katie. I still remembers how your father used to call you his Savannah sparrow."

Katie smiled. "I never knew why he called me that. Mama said it was because Papa knew I would never be contented to stay in one place. He was always afraid I would take off some day."

"The Savannah sparrow is one of the most valuable birds in Labrador," Matt said. "They arrives on the coast in May, stays 'til late October. They lives off weeds and insects. Not like some of the other birds who feeds off our fish."

He pulled Katie close. The feel of his hands on her set her heart pounding. She held herself very still, barely breathing. Then Matt was kissing her, his mouth opening slightly on hers. She felt as if the bottom of her stomach had fallen away. A warmth was spreading inside her like sunshine. "Katie," Matt whispered. "Will you wait for me?"

Wait for him? What did he mean?

"You don't have to decide now," he said, hugging her.

From what seemed like far away, Katie could hear Lucy calling. "We have to go now, Kate. It's almost ten-thirty. Our tram will be leaving soon."

Katie snuggled against Matt, wanting the night to go on forever.

"I have curfew," Lucy was saying.

Reluctantly, Katie pulled away from Matt. "I should

go," she whispered. She would be taking the same tram as Lucy, the one that went up Spring Garden Road before heading to the North End.

Matt pressed a quick kiss to her lips. "I'll write you," he promised.

The tram came shortly, and Matt and George waved from the sidewalk as Lucy and Katie boarded.

"Have a safe trip overseas," Lucy called.

The tram sped away into the dark night, Matt's kiss still warm on Katie's lips, his words echoing in her brain. *Will you wait for me, Katie?*

Chapter 22

AN UNEXPECTED DISCOVERY

"Today, we will begin a new novel," Miss Forster was saying. "*Jane Eyre* by Charlotte Brontë.

Katie was barely listening. She couldn't keep her mind off Matt. The memory of his kiss left her giddy. For the past couple of weeks, she had played and replayed their meeting in her mind. *Wait for me, Katie.* It all seemed unreal now, like a dream. She thought of all the men who came back from the war wounded. Hospital ships carrying wounded men arrived regularly in Halifax. Some didn't return at all. Cholera and typhus were common diseases and a threat to the soldiers. Quickly, Katie brushed those thoughts aside. She had to find Hannah, and she had years of nursing training in front of her. *You will have to wait for me too, Matt Reid.*

Another six weeks and school would be over. Birdie and Miss Storr would be expecting Katie to return to St. Anthony. But how could she leave without Hannah? Whenever she thought of it, she got a sick feeling in her stomach.

Lucy nudged Katie, jolting her back to the present. She had come to school late this morning and Katie had not had a chance to speak with her. Lucy slipped her a note. Katie waited until Miss Forster had her back to the class before she read it. *Kate, Meet me at recess. I have something urgent to tell you.*

Katie read the note twice. A quick glance at the clock on the teacher's desk told her that recess would begin in another twenty minutes. What did Lucy have to tell her that was so urgent?

After what seemed like forever, Miss Forster rang the bell announcing the beginning of recess. Students got out of their desks and began filing outside.

"Lucy MacDougall," Miss Foster said, "I need to see you."

Katie shot Lucy a bewildered look. Lucy shrugged helplessly.

While Katie waited, she read Lucy's words again, noting that *urgent* had been underlined.

She glanced impatiently toward the doorway.

Recess was more than half over by the time Lucy came out into the yard. She grabbed Katie's arm, pulling her over to a maple in front of the school. "I was afraid recess would be over before I had a chance to talk with you."

"What is it, Lucy?"

"Oh, Kate, I could kick myself for misleading you."

Misleading her. What was Lucy trying to tell her?

"Lydia Parker is a friend of John's," she said. "I saw her at church last night." Katie didn't know what this had to do with her, but she let Lucy continue on. "Lydia's sister, Janet, used to work for the Abbotts." Katie nodded, realizing where this was going, impatient now for Lucy to get to the point. "It wasn't Rose Johnson who took your sister." Lucy paused, took a deep breath before continuing. "You see, Kate, Mrs. Abbott had two servants named Rose. Well, actually, the woman who took your sister was *Rosetta*. Rosetta Tate." Lucy ran her fingers through her thick hair. "I wish I had talked with Lydia sooner. I could have saved you a lot of grief and . . ."

"Do you know where Rosetta Tate is?" Katie interrupted, grasping the full impact of what Lucy was telling her.

"Lydia's apartment is in the North End, not far from our house. She may be able to give you information about Rosetta Tate."

Once again, Katie felt a faint stirring of hope.

The bell rang and students came running down from the slopes of the Citadel and in from the street. They were already starting to form a line.

Lucy handed Katie a piece of paper with Lydia Parker's address and phone number. "I can go with you after school if you like."

But Katie was already walking out the gate.

⌒

Less than an hour later, she was sitting in the living room of Lydia Parker's apartment while Lydia put her little boy down for his morning nap.

"There's coffee on the stove. Help yourself," she called from the bedroom.

"I'm fine," Katie called, settling back on the sofa. The room was small with barely enough space for a sofa and an armchair. On a small table was a framed picture of a man in uniform. From the bedroom, she could hear Lydia murmuring soothing sounds to her son.

Feeling jittery, Katie stood up, idly pacing the small room. Her heart told her not to expect too much. After all, Lydia was only the sister of someone who was friends with Rosetta Tate. So many times Katie's hopes had been dashed. Still, she couldn't contain the bubble of anticipation that rose within her. This is definitely a breakthrough, she told herself as she glanced out the window toward the Narrows. Ships of every size and description filled the harbor. Since the war, freighters, tankers, warships, and long lean ships from all over the world entered and left port. Huge convoys often gathered in Halifax to make the voyage overseas. To the right was George's Island, and directly across the harbor was the Nova Scotia Hospital where poor Rose Johnson had to be committed.

Lydia returned shortly. She had taken off her apron, and her hair that had been tied in a bun now hung loose around her freckled face. She didn't look much older than Katie even though she had a toddler and was obviously expecting another child. Katie wondered how she would manage with two small children and a husband away at war.

"Are you sure I can't get you something?" Lydia asked. "Tea? Milk?"

"No, thanks," Katie said. She was eager to find out about Rosetta Tate's whereabouts. "I'm sorry to barge in unannounced."

"I don't know if I can be of much help," Lydia said. "I don't even know where Rosetta is anymore. She married Ed Tate, and I hear he was wounded in the war. They moved away after he came back."

Moved away. Katie felt her initial surge of hope slipping away. "Did yeh ever meet Rosetta?"

"Yes, on a few occasions. We were planning to invite her and her husband, along with Janet and her husband, over for dinner, but then all this happened." She gestured to the harbor with its massive warships and tankers.

"Did she say why she took Hannah?"

Lydia was thoughtful. "It was obvious she loved the little one. And Janet once told me that Rosetta often went to the Abbotts' on her day off just so she could be with Hannah. After she got married, she took Hannah to live with her."

Katie felt a wave of gratitude for this woman who had cared so much for her little sister.

Lydia lowered her voice confidentially. "I heard that Mrs. Abbott was not a good mother at all. Didn't pay much attention to the little girl. Left her with servants most of the time."

Katie's insides twisted.

"Not that Rosetta had all the time in the world," Lydia added. "She spent her evenings at night school, and most of her free time was spent studying."

She rose to her feet and went to a mahogany cabinet in the corner of the room and opened a drawer. She came back with some photographs.

"Rosetta brought Hannah to our Bobby's second birthday party. My brother is a photographer." Lydia sorted through the photographs. "Here's a picture of Hannah and Bobby together."

With trembling hands, Katie reached for the photograph.

"See how our Bobby has his arm around your little sister's shoulder."

Katie's eyes swept eagerly over the photograph. She felt her throat tighten, and the ache in her chest was making it difficult for her to breathe. Hannah's face had lost its chubby baby look. She had turned into a girl. A feeling of loss flooded through Katie.

Lydia rifled through the pictures, finding another one. "Here's a picture of Hannah and Rosetta."

Again, Katie's hand reached out eagerly. This time, she couldn't believe what she was seeing. She gave an audible gasp, the image swimming in front of her.

"Is everything okay?" Lydia hovered over her.

Katie was so taken aback, she couldn't tear her eyes away from the picture.

"What is it, Kate?"

"It's Etta," she finally managed, her eyes still riveted to the photograph. "Etta Duncan."

Chapter 23

SISTERLY DEVOTION

"*Y*ou know her?" Lydia sounded surprised.

Katie nodded. "She's a friend of mine."

"Rosetta did say she knew the child's family." Lydia puckered her forehead as if trying to remember something important. "I thought she told me Hannah's family was dead."

Katie struggled to make sense of it all. Mrs. Abbott must have taken Etta with her to St. John's. Etta had been looking for domestic work. She must have assumed they'd all perished. And of course Hannah would feel comfortable with Etta who had spent hours with her on the Labrador. And Etta, bless her, would not stand to see Hannah unhappy. It was clear now why Etta would take Hannah home with her.

"I have Rosetta's address . . . the address on North Street where she used to live. Maybe the landlord has a forwarding address." Lydia said.

"Thanks," Katie said, handing her the picture.

"You can keep it," Lydia said.

Katie looked up and down the street at the long row of houses on either side. How many times had she walked past this street in the last couple of months? She could feel the sting of tears behind her eyelids. Now Hannah was gone again.

The large two-story house that stood at 780 North had brick siding and the front door had a large oval window of frosted glass. Katie opened the door and stepped into the foyer. The building had been converted into flats, and the tenants' names were listed next to their apartment numbers.

E. Tate was listed next to apartment four, on the second floor. Katie felt a faint stirring of hope. Maybe they hadn't moved yet. She climbed the long curved mahogany staircase and walked down a wide hallway. The door to the apartment was slightly ajar, and she could see a woman on her knees with a scrub bucket. She rose to her feet when she saw Katie. "The flat won't be ready for another week," she said.

All Katie's hopes vanished. "I'm looking for information on Ed and Rosetta Tate," she explained. "They used to live here."

The woman wiped her forehead with the back of her hand. "Mrs. Tate left at the end of the month, right after Mr. Tate got wounded in the war. Her father's not well, and she decided to go home."

"Back to the Labrador?"

The woman shrugged. "Wherever it is they're from. She took the little one and left. Her husband will be joining her, I presume." She shook her head. "So many of them coming back wounded nowadays."

Katie nodded absently.

"I was sorry to see them go," the woman said. "They were such good tenants, and the little girl was so sweet. She used to wave to me from the window whenever she saw me."

Katie swallowed over the lump in her throat.

At least Hannah's safe, Katie told herself as she walked home. Etta will take good care of her. Hannah had not fallen into the hands of evil people as Katie had feared. She shuddered, remembering the rooming house on Hollis Street.

"What's wrong?" Gwen asked when Katie walked through the door, and Katie knew the distress on her face must have been obvious.

"I found Hannah," she said, and letting herself sink into the comfort of a wing chair, she gave herself over to weeping.

"Are you all right?" Gwen asked with some alarm.

Katie nodded, but continued to cry. She felt relief that her sister was with Etta. But she felt sadness too, as she thought of the picture Lydia had given her. Hannah had grown from a baby into a little girl, and Katie had missed those years.

"Hannah is with Etta," she told Gwen. "My friend from the Labrador." She showed Gwen the photograph, explaining that Etta came to Halifax to be a servant for the Abbotts. Katie smiled through her tears. "At least Hannah's not lost anymore."

Gwen put an arm around Katie's shoulder. "I'm happy for you," she said. "I know the relief you must feel." She rose from the sofa and went to stand by the window. She stared out at the street for a few moments, before turning to face Katie. "I have found my sister too," she said glancing toward the mahogany table.

Katie followed her gaze to the framed picture of Julia that had been taken out of the drawer. She could only stare at Gwen. "Was she lost?" she asked finally.

Gwen began pacing the room. "In a way, yes."

Katie waited for her to continue.

"Julia and I have not spoken for years. I didn't even know where she was until last evening. We quarrelled before I left England, you see. Julia stole the man I loved." Gwen gave a humorless laugh. "The man I *thought* I loved," she amended. "We quarrelled, and when I left England, I didn't leave a forwarding address. I wanted nothing more to do with Julia." Gwen sat down on the sofa beside Katie. "As years passed, I realized how much I missed my sister. I wrote to her in England, but by that time she had left the country. I learned from a cousin that she had moved to the United States." Gwen sighed. "It wasn't until you started looking for Hannah that I began to see what I had truly lost . . . thrown away really. I decided then to search for Julia, and I found out she's in New York, married." Gwen smiled. "Not to the scoundrel who left me. She has a child, a little boy, Nathan, who is almost three. They are coming to visit me this summer."

"That's great," Katie said. "I'm happy for you."

"It was because of you, Katie, that I reconciled with Julia again." Gwen smiled at her. "Your devotion to your sisters really touched something in me. You taught me how not to take family for granted."

Kate recalled Gwen's strange behavior, the way she looked eagerly through the mail when it was delivered. "Why didn't you tell me you were searching for Julia?"

Gwen shrugged. "I guess it was because I didn't have much hope of finding her." She touched Katie's shoulder. "What a burden we've both carried."

"Yes," Katie agreed.

Gwen peered at her. "What will you do now?"

"There's only one thing to do," Katie said. "I'm going back to the Labrador."

Chapter 24

JUNE 19-15

"*I* don't see any snow," a passenger commented, as the *Prospero* drew nearer to port.

"Where are all the Eskimos?" another man asked. He raised his binoculars and gazed at the sloping hills in the distance, dark green with moss and scrub growth.

Katie smiled, remembering stories she'd heard about tourists arriving on the Labrador coast in the middle of summer carrying skis and snowshoes, expecting to find igloos and Eskimos dressed in furs.

As houses, buildings, and fish stages grew three-dimensional, passengers came to lean against the ship's railing. They shielded their eyes with their hands to get a better look. Katie saw that a cluster of people had gathered on the landwash near a small dock. She wondered if Ruth was among them. Her sister was getting passage on the *Strathcona* and was scheduled to arrive in Labrador around the same time as Katie.

As the *Prospero's* chains rattled down, Katie slowly let out her breath. Gwen had wanted her to finish the school term, but Katie was eager be return to Labrador. It had been nearly nine months since she left Ruth at the children's home, and Hannah had been missing for over eighteen months now. Miss Foster had arranged for Katie to write the exam early, and although she wouldn't get the results until the end of the summer, she felt certain she had done well.

Katie looked out toward the lofty cliffs, at the shrieking seagulls hovering above the water. So many people had been kind to her. Gwen had wired the mission, and they were able to find Katie a position as a nurse's aide at the Carney Bay nursing station. Ada Cameron, the nurse in charge, had worked with Gwen at St. Anthony's hospital. Ada loved children, Gwen had told Katie, and she was sympathetic to Katie's predicament. Ada had suggested that Katie use the caretaker's cottage attached to the nursing station. He had retired, and the man taking his place had a family and a home in the village.

The ship's whistle gave a loud, short blast, startling Katie out of her thoughts. A little while later, a lifeboat was lowered into the water, and Katie was rowed ashore by a member of the crew. As the boat drew toward land, she scanned the people on the landwash hoping to get a glimpse of Ruth.

She was greeted on the dock by a heavyset woman wearing a white apron over a cotton dress, her light brown hair encased in a hair net. "You must be Kate," she said, holding out her hand.

"Kate Andrews." She took the woman's outstretched hand.

"I'm Annie. I cooks the meals for the staff and patients at the station."

"Pleased to meet yeh," Katie said, her eyes still searching the crowd for Ruth. "Did the *Strathcona* arrive?"

Annie shook her head. "We don't expect her 'til tomorrow." She gave Katie a sidelong glance. "Nurse Cameron tells me you're expectin' yer sister."

Katie nodded. "Ruth. She's seven. I thought she would have arrived by now."

"She'll be here tomorrow, I'm sure," Annie said reassuringly. She took Katie's elbow. "Come with me, now. Sam will collect yer luggage when he picks up the supplies that's come in for the mission. The station's this way." She pointed to a cluster of houses built on a ridge.

For the next few minutes, they walked in silence. After weeks at sea, Katie found it hard to steady herself. Her legs felt as unsteady as a newborn calf's. The ground pitched beneath her, and she was having difficulty balancing her knees.

"Nurse Cameron went over to Bakeapple Bight on the *Yale*." Annie said after a while. "There's a man over there in a wonderful bad way. Don't know what we'll do if she brings the poor soul back with her. He'll have to sleep on the floor." She pushed back a strand of hair that had escaped from her hairnet. "Since the fishin' boats come down from Newfoundland, we've been filled to the rafters. Good thing some of the patients is ready to go home." She looked at Katie. "Nurse tells me you'll be goin' over to Shelter Bay tomorrow on the *Yale* to get yeh other sister."

"That's right." Katie had been wondering how she would get to Shelter Bay where Etta's family lived, but it looked as if everything had been arranged.

"The Broomfield baby is ready to go home. You can take care of him on the trip. It'll save one of us from havin' to go." They had reached the top of a steep hill, and Annie was panting from the exertion of the climb.

"This way," she said, leading Katie toward an L-shaped, one-story building built against the shelter of a large cliff overlooking the ocean. Katie followed her through what she guessed was a waiting area. The wood floor was well scrubbed, and the room had the antiseptic smell of hospitals. The ceiling had open rafters with large beams running across. A middle-aged man was sitting on a wooden bench against one wall.

"What ails you now, Charl?" Annie asked.

"I wants me toot' hauled," the man replied, his hand automatically going to his jaw.

"Nurse is gone off in the *Yale*. Don't know when she'll be gettin' back."

"I'll wait," he said grimly.

Annie made a face. "That's Charlie Pike," she whispered, as she led Katie up three steps and down a lengthy hallway. "Achin' Charl, we calls him. Comes in here nearly every day with some kind of ache or pain. Got the poor nurse drove right mental."

Katie followed Annie into a long kitchen with rows of cupboards and a large wooden table. Like the waiting area, the ceiling in this room was not enclosed. A young woman with a white kerchief tied over her dark curly hair was standing over a big iron stove stirring a pot of steaming stew. The yeasty aroma of baking bread filled Katie's nostrils.

"This is Myra Obed," Annie said, "a wop from the States. She helps out with just about everyt'ing around here."

"I'm very pleased to meet you," Katie said, grasping Myra's hand. She knew wops were workers without pay. Every summer dozens of them came from Canada, England, and the United States to volunteer at the mission. Birdie often said Dr. Grenfell could talk people into anything. Over the years, doctors, dentists, teachers, and ditch diggers gave up their vacations to come work for him.

Myra smiled, showing teeth that were slightly protruding. "Please sit down," she said, gesturing to one of the kitchen chairs.

Katie liked Myra's warm, cheerful manner. Her slow, easy way of talking reminded her of Miss Carleton back in Fathom Harbour.

"I tells Myra that before she leaves here, she'll be able to do most of the things the nurse can." Annie had put the kettle on and was measuring tea into the teapot. "That goes for you too, Kate. Nurse Cameron will expect yeh to bandage cuts, wash and dress patients, and help newborn babies. By the time yeh goes into nursin', you'll already know half the stuff they'll try to learn yeh."

"Gwen told me I'll get the practical experience I needs," Katie said proudly.

"Don't s'pose yeh knows how to handle a dog team. We needs someone to drive Nurse Cameron in the winter." Anne lifted the damper and shoved a large junk of wood in the stove. "Got nine fine huskies out back. Young Joe Goudie down in the bay used to be our driver before he went off to war."

"I can handle a dog team fine," Katie told her. "My father taught me."

"That so?" Annie's eyes raked over Katie's thin frame. "It's not somet'ing I can do," she said, looking down at her own massive bulk.

Katie knew that weight meant everything when it came to dog travel; it was not a job for a heavy person like Annie.

"I won't mind driving the nurse," Katie said. "Not at all." In fact, she knew that when winter came, she would be happy to get out into the bracing cold air. In Labrador, no one could travel far in winter without a dog team.

"I can't wait to experience my first winter in Labrador," Myra said, breezily. She had been listening intently to the conversation between Annie and Katie.

"You're stayin' the winter?" Katie asked, surprised. Most volunteers usually stayed only for the summer months.

Myra told her she had attended one of Dr. Grenfell's lectures in Boston. "I was really impressed," she said. "However, it was after reading his book,

Adrift on an Ice Pan, that I knew I just had to come to Labrador."

Katie wondered if anyone had prepared Myra for the harsh winters on the coast. Gwen once said that sometimes doctors and nurses came to work at the mission with their heads filled with romantic notions and no idea of what they really faced. They soon learned that temperatures could drop to below forty degrees, and traveling by dog team could be painfully slow. When the last coastal boat left in the fall, they could be cut off from the outside world for as long as six months. After a few months, they longed for running water, electricity, newspapers, and the conveniences of city life.

"I'll show yeh where you'll be sleeping," Annie said, rousing Katie out of her musings. "Myra, while the tea is steeping, would yeh heat up them tea biscuits I made for lunch?"

"Of course," Myra said, as Annie led Katie to her accommodations at the back of the building.

"Not much space," Annie said, looking around the sparsely furnished rooms. "It was built for a single person."

"It's fine," Katie said, looking around her. There were two rooms, both sparsely furnished. The other room had a single bed, a table, a chair, and a potbellied stove. On a stand in a corner was a jug and basin for washing.

"Yous'll be taking your meals with us," Annie told her. "I'll find yeh some sheets and blankets later," she promised. "But let's go and have somet'ing to eat, now. Yer probably hungry after such a long cruise."

Shortly after the *Prospero* left, the mission boat *Yale* arrived. From the window, Katie could see her weathered gray sails billowing in the slight breeze. She watched as a lifeboat was lowered from the deck.

"There seems to be only the nurse and the skipper," Annie said, as the boat approached the dock. "They must have left the patient behind. But what's that the nurse got in her arms?"

As Ada Cameron got closer, Katie saw that she was a tall graceful woman with short curly red hair. She was wearing rubber boots that reached the hem of her cotton dress. It wasn't until she came inside, that they realized the bundle in her arms was a baby.

She looked around the room, her eyes falling on Katie. "You made it, lass," she said. "Sorry I couldn't be on hand to meet you, but I hope you are making yourself at home."

"Thank-you," Katie said. She recognized the nurse's accent as Scottish. She had met a number of Scottish people during her stay at St. Anthony's hospital.

"Who's this then?" Annie asked, touching the tuft of black hair on top of the baby's head. The baby lifted his head and stared at her with large dark eyes.

"This is young Master McNeil," the nurse explained. "The poor wee thing has a bit of a chest rattle, and I dinna like the sound of it. Afraid it might turn into pneumonia." She frowned. "His house is so dank and damp, and his wee feet were red with cold when I found him. Tomorrow, I'll have Dr. Grenfell take a peek at him." She jiggled the baby. "But isn't he the bonnie lad? I bet his Mama misses him terrible."

"All the cribs is filled up," Annie said. "S'pose I'll have to get Sam to bring that apple crate in from the shed. Maybe he can rig somet'ing up." She looked at Katie. "We makes do with what we has around here."

Nurse Cameron took off her sweater and hung it on a hook by the door. "How is everyone?" she inquired.

"Mrs. Hope is still in a wonderful bad way," Annie told her, "although the baby seems to be doin' fine. And I was able to get Mr. Pottle to eat a little. Mr. Simpson is gone out for a walk. He's right restless now that he's feelin' better. Anxious to get back at the cod, he is."

The nurse handed the baby to Myra. "Mr. Pike is in

the waiting room waiting to have a tooth pulled," she said. She turned to Katie. "We'll have a wee chat later, lass. Soon as I have some free time. Maybe this evening." She smiled. "After tomorrow you will be really busy, what with starting a new job and two little girls to care for."

Katie's heart soared. *Two* little girls to care for.

Chapter 25

RETURN TO THE TICKLE

*S*leep did not come easy for Katie that night. She twisted and turned in the narrow bed, and it was hours before she finally dozed off. When she awoke a few hours later, the sky was streaked with silver, gold, and pink light. From outside her bedroom window, she could hear the chirp of robins and a Savannah sparrow singing an early morning song.

Katie got out of bed, got dressed and went to the kitchen. The fires were already lit and Annie was standing at the stove cooking oatmeal. Although she wasn't expected to start work until the following day, Katie helped Annie cook breakfast, and helped feed the patients. It gave her something to do and helped take her mind off Hannah.

Shortly after seven, Fred Blake, the *Yale's* skipper, came to the nursing station to fetch patients who were ready to go home. The *Yale* was anchored in the harbor, her skiff tied to the dock. Annie dressed little Geordie and handed him to Katie. "Make sure he keeps his cap on," she cautioned. "It gets right cold out there on the water."

Annie packed cheese and bread for them to eat on the journey. She filled a bottle with goat's milk for the baby. At a quarter to eight, Katie walked down to the beach, carrying the baby. Mr. Simpson and another patient followed behind them. Two men in rubber boots were waiting on the dock. The skipper explained they would be traveling with them to a fishing station along the way.

It was a beautiful morning with brilliant sunshine, a cloudless sky, and only the hint of a breeze. Skillfully, Skipper Fred sailed the *Yale* into bays and channels, bights and tickles, dropping off patients and supplies. A pleasant man, he kept up a steady flow of conversation. The *Yale*, he told Katie, was donated to the mission by a group of students from a famous university in the United States. She was used to fetch and return patients between hospitals and nursing stations. To help maintain her cost, she had a contract to carry mail and supplies as well as any chance passengers. Most of the skipper's time was spent at Indian Harbour Hospital, where he sailed the doctor to widely scattered hamlets along the coast. The doctor treated the minor cases, bringing the more severe to the hospital.

It was almost noon by the time the skipper rowed the last passenger ashore. "Where to?" he asked Katie after he returned to the *Yale*. "Shelter Harbour or Nellie's Tickle?"

"Let's try the Tickle first," she said. She wondered if Etta's family still went there to fish. There was even a good chance Etta might be with them.

As soon as the Yale dropped anchor, people came running out of their huts and down to the water's edge. As she climbed down the rope ladder, Katie was reminded of all the times she and Etta rushed to the landwash whenever a boat came into the harbor. That seemed like such a long time ago, now. Katie could feel her heart pounding as the boat drew nearer to shore.

She was not prepared for the reception she got from the people on the beach. They stood in clusters, staring open-mouthed. Although all eyes were on her as the skipper helped her out of the skiff, no one spoke, waved or even smiled.

"Oh, my Gawd!" Maud Skinner said, breaking the silence. "Oh, my Gawd! It's Katie come back," and before she could say anything, Maud was crushing her in a hug. "Where yeh been to, my dear? We heard yous had all perished."

"Only Mama and Papa," Katie said, feeling a fresh wave of pain.

Maud's features softened. "I'm sorry, my love."

A number of people moved toward her then. A little boy shyly offered her a piece of hard tack. Some of the other women were dabbing at their eyes. "Bless you, dear," one lady said, and Katie saw that she was crying. It dawned on her that they all thought she was dead.

"What brings yeh back to the tickle?" Maud asked.

"I'm lookin' for Etta Duncan." Katie scanned the faces in the crowd. There were new faces mixed in with the familiar ones, but Etta was not among them.

"None of the Duncans is here this season," Maud said. "And I haven't seen Etta for two years now. I heard she moved to the mainland."

"Two of her brothers enlisted in the war," said someone from the crowd.

"A lot of young people is gone off to war," Maud said. She shook her head. "Don't know what England's ever done for we people that we should sacrifice our sons and husbands. Come," she told Katie, "let's go talk to Aunt Jane. If anyone knows where Etta's to, it'll be she. Right now, she's tendin' to me sister Meg."

Katie followed Maud away from the throng of people. By this time, most of the children had lost interest and had moved away. The skipper stayed behind to talk with some of the people on the beach.

They picked their way along a web of paths that looped along the shore. Katie noticed that many of the huts were boarded up.

"Not as many people comes here now," Maud explained. "And I can't say I blames them. Since the war, the price of fish dropped so low that most of the time we works for nothin'." She shook her head. "We all felt the pinch of hunger last winter. People nearly starved to death. And I can't see it gettin' no better."

Katie felt a pang, but said nothing.

After walking a little while longer, her footsteps slowed. Katie could see their old summer home in the distance. It looked smaller than she remembered it.

"Go take a peek if you needs to," Maud said, as if reading her mind.

Katie's knees felt weak as she entered the small building. It was cold and dark with patches of ice in the corners. The heavy odor of dampness and mold stung her nostrils. Old memories flickered to life, bringing a smart of tears. Her father's plaid shirt hung on a nail on the wall. A fish net he had been working on still clung to a hook in the corner. Dishes and pots were just as her mother had left them. The wooden doll Papa had made for Hannah was face down on the floor. A sense of loss swept through Katie, as she bent to pick it up. She held the doll to her chest, grief filling all her hollow places. The sadness would always be there, she realized. All it took was a memory to bring it all back again. She closed the cabin door, shutting out the memories of her past.

"Are yeh okay?" Maud asked, patting her shoulder.

Katie nodded, clutching the doll. "It's a shame for the cabin to go to ruin," she said. "When the fishing gets back to normal, I would like for some family to take it over."

"Good idea," Maud said, as they made their way down the beach.

Maud's sister's sod hut stood at a distance from the others. "Aunt Jane," as everyone called her, was standing over a battered pot. She was midwife and medicine woman, and when there was no other medical aid available, she treated the fishermen and their families with plants, roots, herbs, and poultices. Her eyes widened in alarm when she saw Katie, but she quickly composed herself.

"Come in, my dear," she said. "Good to see yeh. Hello, Maud."

Even before Katie crossed the threshold, she was aware of the heavy scent of damp earth. A dim light fell through a tiny window created from various pieces of glass. She took a seat on one of the benches around a rough wooden table. Six bunks were built against the wall, fashioned after the model of berths on ships. It was so dark inside that at first Katie didn't notice the woman under the pile of rags in the lower bunk until she let out a low moan.

"How is yeh, Meg?" Maud asked, moving quickly to her sister's side.

"Got a wonderful pain in me stumick," the woman said, struggling to sit up. Katie could see that she was pale and gaunt, her arms so thin they looked like laths nailed to her shoulders.

Maud crossed her arms over her chest. "Got her gut ruined, that one," she said to no one in particular. "I keeps tellin' her she got to eat more, but she won't listen to nobody. She'll be no use to her youngsters if she starves to death."

"The *Strathcona* is expected today," Katie told them. "Maybe yer sister could sail back with us to Carney Bay nursing station."

"I can't leave me youngsters."

"G'wan maid. I'll look after the youngsters," Maud told her. "You're some lucky Katie and the skipper come today. It'll likely be days 'fore the doctor gets a chance to call here."

Ignoring her sister's protests, Maud walked around the room picking up Meg's things and stuffing them into a flour sack.

"What brings yeh back to the Tickle, Katie?" Aunt Jane asked.

"She's lookin' for Etta Duncan," Maud answered for her.

"The Duncans moved further north," Aunt Jane told her. "Poor Felix, that's Etta's father, had a stroke. He's gettin' up in age, poor old feller."

A great hard lump rose in Katie's throat. "Where'd they move to?"

"Nobody knows. A lot of families is after leavin'. Hard to make a livin' here anymore." She laughed as she measured out tea. "Soon there won't be nobody left but me and the gulls."

Katie refused the offer of tea from Aunt Jane, and while Maud bustled around the hut, helping her sister get ready for the voyage, Katie concentrated on a spot on the wall, willing herself not to cry. God knows when she'd get to see Hannah again.

Katie's heart was heavy as she walked back to the boat, her eyes burning with unshed tears. *Hannah's with Etta,* she reminded herself. *She's safe.* She tried not to think of the thousands of families living in the scattered bays, inlets, coves, and tickles along

Labrador's jagged coast. Etta and Hannah could be anywhere.

"I'll keep me eyes open," the skipper told Katie, after they had rowed back to the *Yale*. He patted Katie's arm. "I'll ask around. I'll talk to Dr. Paddon at North West River, and I'll contact the Hudson Bay Company."

"Thank-you," Katie said, comforted by his kindness.

It was nearly four o'clock when the *Yale* rounded the point at Carney Bay. There was still no sign of the *Strathcona*.

Annie was waiting for them on the dock. She glanced at the doll Katie held in her hand. "No luck?"

Katie shook her head, not trusting herself to speak.

"I'm sorry, dear," Annie said.

"The *Strathcona* didn't come?"

"They'll be here by and by. Knowin' the doctor, he'll be pokin' into every little cove and bay along the way. And if there's sick people he'll tend to them before movin' on. The doctor's always late." She laughed. "The late Dr. Grenfell, we calls him."

Annie glanced toward the dory where Skipper Fred was helping Meg out of the boat. "Looks like the skipper could use some help," she said, moving toward them.

Katie went straight to her room and lay on her bed fully dressed. *I'll find Hannah,* she promised herself before giving over to the tears she had been holding in all afternoon.

She couldn't remember drifting off to sleep, but a light rap on the door awakened her. The shadows of evening were gathering outside her window, filling the corners of her room. She had slept through supper. Annie opened the door and poked her head in. "The *Strathcona's* comin' in the harbor," she said. "We can see her lights from the window."

Katie got up from the bed, pulled on a sweater, and hurried down to the dock to wait.

It was dark by the time the *Strathcona* dropped anchor. Kerosene lamps had been lit, casting long rectangles of light on the ground outside the windows. By this time the wind had picked up, and as Katie waited on the dock, she could hear the waves slapping against the rough boards of the dock.

Annie came to stand beside her, a lantern in her hand. The ship's searchlight swept in wide arcs, slicing circles in the darkness. Katie could hear disembodied voices carrying on the calm water. The deck lights came on illuminating every detail of the ship. She watched as a jolly boat was lowered into the water. Someone was helping a small figure down the rope ladder. Katie's heart thumped with excitement.

The searchlight cut a golden path across the dark water. It shone on the jolly boat illuminating the passengers and crew members. Dr. Grenfell was sitting beside Ruth, a scuffed black bag on his lap, his gray hair tousled from the wind. Katie was reminded of the evening Gwen took her to a play at the garrison in Halifax. She recalled how the bright lights came up on the actors. The people in the jolly boat reminded her of characters in a play. Dr. Grenfell leaned forward, whispered something to Ruth, and she began to wave. Katie saw that most of her front teeth were missing.

Katie began to wave too, although she knew Ruth couldn't see her. "Ruth," she called. "Ruth, it's me, Katie."

She kept waving and calling her sister's name, until Ruth was in her arms, Katie hugging her close.

Chapter 26

A SURPRISE VISITOR

August 25, 1915

Dearest Matt:

I was happy to get your last letter, although it makes me sad to think of you being cold all the time. It must be nerve-racking to be constantly shot at. A lot of men on the Labrador coast have volunteered to go to war. Annie says she can't see the sense in it. Lucy wrote that her brother, John, came home wounded. It will be some time before he is able to walk again.

Summer passed in a blur of activity, and now the moss on the hills is showing the first signs of fall. Soon the Savannah sparrows will take flight. I am still searching for Hannah, and not a day goes by that I don't think of her. We will soon be into the stand still months—those months when there is not enough snow for dog travel and where travel by boat is too hazardous. If I do not find Hannah soon, I will have to wait until late spring. It is disheartening to think that I will have to wait so long to see her again.

The good news is that I passed my examinations. Passed with flying colors, as Gwen put it.

When I find Hannah, I will either go to St. John's or back to Halifax to do my training. But right now, I am needed on the coast. The Moravian missionaries, because they are German, have all been deported. Annie says she never heard tell of such foolishness in all her life. I too find it hard to understand why they would deport those kind, gentle people who have done so much good. The people in the north are suffering because of it. It has put a burden on the mission. A lot of doctors and nurses have joined the forces, and Dr. Grenfell will soon be leaving.

Ruth has settled in well, and has made friends with the other children. Helen Graham, the caretaker's wife, is a schoolteacher from Mill Town. She has offered to teach Ruth in the fall, along with her own three children and the children in the bay. Since we do not have a schoolhouse, she will be using the parlor here at the nursing station.

Our station is a small, drafty building without running water or electricity. We bring our drinking water from the lake in buckets. Come winter, we will have to chop holes in the ice and melt snow to bathe the patients and do the laundry.

I have learned to apply bandages to cuts, to treat burns and boils, and I often assist Nurse Cameron with delivering babies. Only the difficult cases, of course—breech births and babies that come before their time. The midwife is quite capable of handling all the others. Just yesterday, a man came to the station with two of his fingers chopped off. Myra, a wop from the States, took full charge. Her parents want her to become a teacher, but since coming to live on the Labrador, she is determined to study nursing. She intends to return to Labrador after she is finished her schooling. Matt, I hate to admit this, but seeing that man with his fingers missing really shook me up. Sometimes I wonder if I have what it takes to make a good nurse. Annie tells me I will do just fine, and it is only natural that I should have doubts. One thing I am sure of is that being a nurse is what I want more than anything else in the world.

Ruth asked me just last evening what does

*Hannah look like now, and it made me sad that
Ruth can no longer remember her sister. I long for
the day when we can be a family again.*

*Matt, I do hope the war will be over soon, and
you will be able to come home.*

Love,
Katie

The days blended one into the other. September
slipped by in a golden haze of Indian summer days.
October brought blustery days and icy winds from in
across the bay. Days grew short, the weather cold and
rough. The Savannah sparrows stopped singing and
disappeared. The coastal boat made her last trip for
the season, her whistle as mournful as a bugle at a
funeral service.

The fishing vessels left the coast to sail back to
Newfoundland, and although there weren't as many
patients now, there was still much to do. Fires had to
be lit, meals prepared, patients washed and fed, floors
scrubbed, and bedding and laundry taken care of.

Slab ice that had been drifting relentlessly up and
down the bay, found its way into the sheltered water
of the cove. Shortly afterward came the first snow of
the season, and by late October winter settled in with
a vengeance. Temperatures dropped to minus

degrees, and northwest winds drove snow into five-foot drifts.

All through the long winter, Katie travelled with Nurse Cameron, the dogs breaking trails over hills, through entangling bush, and over snow banks and ballicaters. Wherever she went, Katie inquired about Etta Duncan, but no one had seen her for over two years.

March came and went, and Katie waited eagerly for spring breakup. By April, the cold lessened, but lakes, ponds, and the ocean were still frozen over.

Toward the end of the month, the nurse got an emergency call. A baby in Tilt cove had come down with pneumonia. She and Katie set out by dog team early the next morning, travelling more than twenty-five miles. They left Tilt Cove the following day, stopping in bays and hamlets along the way. Nurse Cameron pulled teeth, gave out medicine, pills, and advice. In the afternoon, they returned to the nursing station.

Katie was tired, and wanted only to sit by the fire, put her feet up and rest. She could hear the children in the parlor, chatting and laughing. It was Friday; lessons had finished for the week, and as a reward, Myra had made them molasses taffy.

So when the knock came at the door that afternoon in late April, the last person Katie expected to see was Jimmy Duncan. In fact, she was beginning to think that all the Duncans had dropped from the face of the earth. But now Etta's cousin was standing before her covered in snow.

⌐

"Are you okay, Miss?" he asked, his voice filled with concern.

Katie realized she was gripping his arm, and she let go, embarrassed.

"Where's Etta?" she asked, her mouth dry.

"Since she come back from the big city, she likes to be called *Rosetta*, her proper name." A smile tugged at Jimmy's lips.

"But . . . where *is* she?" Katie asked again, a note of impatience creeping into her voice. "I have searched endlessly. Somebody told me she moved north."

"Etta's in the san in St. John's," Jimmy said, his tone serious now. "Been there for almost a year. TB, Miss."

"Is she going to be okay?" Katie asked anxiously. She knew tuberculosis was a serious illness; sometimes patients didn't recover.

"I hope so, Miss," Jimmy said. "We never gives up

hope."

"Do yeh know where my sister is? Hannah Andrews. Etta brought Hannah back from Canada after her husband was wounded in the war."

Jimmy stared at her. "Yeh see, Miss, young Hannah is one of the youngsters that took sick."

Katie felt her pulse quicken. "Hannah's in Fox's Cove? She's been in the cove all this time?"

"Come there a few months ago with me cousin Dodie—that's Etta's sister. They took the youngster in after Etta got too sick to look after her."

"Hannah . . ." Katie said, her voice wobbly, " . . . is she very sick?"

"A fever, Miss. Could be nothin' a'tall to it," Jimmy added after seeing Katie's stricken look. "Yeh knows what youngsters is like. Sometimes they snaps right out of it."

Katie looked out the window at the swirling snow. There were still a few hours of daylight left. She could easily get to Job's Inlet before dark and get a head start in the morning.

"Too dirty out to go anywheres now, Miss." Jimmy said, as if reading her thoughts. "Best to wait 'til mornin'. That way me dogs'll get a chance to rest."

"You and Nurse Cameron can start out tomorrow," Katie told him. "I'm leavin' now."

Chapter 27

APRIL 1916

"But surely Miss . . . it's more than twenty miles. And in this weather."

"Annie," Katie called, and moments later Annie appeared in the doorway. "I'm going out," Katie announced. "Soon as I gets the dogs fed."

Annie glanced out the window. "Yer goin' out in this weather? By your own self?"

"I have to," Katie said. "Hannah's in Fox's Cove." She glanced at Jimmy who was still standing over the stove. "This is Jimmy Duncan, Etta's cousin."

"Better get that wet coat off, my son," Annie said. "Don't want yeh catchin' pneumonia." She turned to face Katie. "Nobody goes nowheres in weather like this without a travelling companion. Anyt'ing can happen. What if yeh falls and breaks a leg?"

Katie watched as Annie filled the kettle, using water from a bucket on the counter. "I'm only goin' as far as

Pigeon Inlet," she said. "If the weather gets too bad, I can always stop at one of the tilts along the way."

Annie took Jimmy's coat, her mouth set in a grim line. "Sit down, my dear, whilst I boils the kettle." To Katie, she said: "I knows there's no use tryin' to talk yeh out of it, Katie, but I'm worried. Somet'ing bad is sure to happen."

Ignoring Annie's grim predictions, Katie went to get the komatic box. Annie rattled off the names of every person on the Labrador coast who got lost in a snowstorm during the last twenty years.

Twenty minutes later, Katie was ready to begin her journey. "Ou-ishet," she shouted, and Thor, her head dog, took the lead, his breath rising like wisps vapor in the chilly winter air. Behind him, harnessed one in front of the other were Dodger, Nellie, Trotter and Jake.

For two hours, Katie guided the dogs along a narrow, twisting trail. A strong breeze drove clouds of snow in her face, blinding her vision. Her eyes stung from the cold. She gripped the sides of the komatic with both hands, colliding with tree trunks and rocks. Her feet were so cold, she could no longer feel her toes. At times, she had to put on snowshoes, and walk ahead of the dogs to beat a path. *Someday, I will be able to hold my own clinics along the coast,* she thought. Now that she'd found Hannah, she could return to

Halifax. She had saved all the money from her job at the nursing station. That, along with her inheritance from Aunt Til would be enough to see her through her years of training. Winter can't last forever, she told herself. Even here in Labrador, spring always comes. In time, the ice will leave the harbor, the sun will shine and flowers will bloom. The Savannah sparrow will come again, and before it takes flight, she would be gone too.

Katie was so deep in thought, she paid little attention to the darkening sky. Now she realized with some alarm that darkness was closing in on her. The trees, dogs, even the snowdrifts, were fading into shadows. The next village was more than two miles away, too far to reach before dark. The snow was too soft to build an igloo. Her only hope was to find the tilt before it got completely dark. She couldn't shake her feelings of uneasiness, knowing that many travellers lost their lives by dropping over a cliff in a snowstorm. She worried that she might have already passed the tilt. It was a low building, and when covered with snow could easily be mistaken for a massive snowbank.

The dogs trotted along in the gathering darkness. They were tired; Katie could tell by their drooping tails and heavy panting. The only other sound was the whish of the komatic's runners on the soft snow. After a while, they came to an abrupt stop, and Katie realized Thor was leading them off the trail.

"Thor, stop!" she cried. But then she saw the tilt nestled in a grove in the trees, its crooked stovepipes sticking through the roof. "Good job, Thor!" She called. "You found the tilt." Nurse Cameron often said Thor was smarter than most humans.

Within minutes, Katie had the dogs out of their harness. She hauled the komatic box inside the tilt, and began unpacking her gear. She found matches, lit a candle, and glanced around the softly shadowed room. The stove was a rusty oil drum, fitted with pipes that went through a hole cut in the roof. The only other furniture was a small wooden table with two large round spruce stumps for chairs. The last person who used the tilt had left behind a large supply of wood.

Before long, Katie had a roaring fire going. She found cheese, bread, and moose stew in the komatic box. She melted snow for drinking water, filling the kettle many times before she had enough water for just one cup of tea. She cradled the steaming cup in her hands, liking the way it warmed her fingers, spreading warmth through her body.

After she had eaten, she spread her sleeping bag on

the floor. Feeling warm and relaxed and pleasantly tired, she drifted off to sleep.

During the night she got up many times to stoke the fire. Outside, the wind was shrill as it whistled down the chimney and under the tilt. Katie arose again at dawn, to find that it was still snowing. The huskies were asleep beneath the snow, their thick fur protecting them from the cold.

The blizzard continued throughout the morning, forcing her to hold up in the tilt. When the dogs were hungry, they came out from under the snow, and she fed them pieces of seal meat. After a while they settled down again, noses tucked under their thick tails.

By noon it was still snowing, but the wind had died down. Katie put the dogs in their harness and started again on her journey. The snow was deep, making it hard for them to pull, and they strained against the heavy load.

After some time she arrived at the shore, the vast whiteness of the frozen sea stretching for miles in the distance. Katie knew she could make better progress traveling over the sea ice than along the narrow trails on land. She also knew spring was an unpredictable time for traveling over the frozen sea. It was never clear how safe the ice was. It could break up without warning, and there was always the danger of having it go abroad, cutting her off from shore. She would travel on the ice, she decided, but stick close to the shoreline. That way, if the ice was bad, she could always leave and go back to land.

After following the shoreline for nearly two hours, Katie came to a long neck of land that jutted out into the sea. By crossing the ice here, she could shorten the distance. She could reach Hannah in less than an hour. But to follow the shoreline all the way around, would increase her time by three, even four, hours. Katie knew it was likely that the rain and the mild weather had weakened the ice. But she was anxious to see Hannah again, and it was already getting late. She had medicine in the komatic box that could benefit not only Hannah, but other patients as well.

"I'll take a chance," Katie said, speaking her thoughts aloud. "I'll take a chance and cross over."

Unhitching the dogs, she put them into a fan-shaped harness, where every dog had its own trace. "Ou-ishet," she shouted, and they leapt forward at once. After a few minutes, they settled into a steady trot across the bay.

Somewhere in the middle of the harbor, Katie became aware that the komatic was moving in a wave-like motion. She had hit rubber ice—a thick slob, not quite frozen. Papa often told her that the best way to keep from falling through slob ice was to keep the komatic moving.

"Ou-ishet," she shouted again, and the dogs picked up speed. They were travelling at a good pace when Dodger, her youngest dog, lay down on the ice. The other dogs tried to keep running, but Dodger was holding them back.

"C'mon Dodger," Katie urged. "C'mon boy." But the dog wouldn't budge.

Katie could feel the back of the komatic sinking into the ice. Water spurted around her. At any minute, she expected the sled to go under. Fear gripped her. There was not a moment to lose. Struggling to keep calm, she held the harness with one hand, and reached inside the komatic box with the other. She found a knife and with one quick movement, cut the dog's trace.

Immediately, the other dogs picked up speed, and the komatic clattered across the rough ice. "C'mon, Dodger," she called, worried that the dog might not find his way.

After a while, Katie could see houses in the distance. They were just specks along the rugged coastline, but hope filled her like a candle in the darkness. She was almost there. As the dogs drew nearer, she could barely contain her joy. Soon, she would be with Hannah.

Katie had almost reached the shore when she saw

something that caught and held her attention. Ahead of her, the ice was broken. From a distance, it looked like a rip in a white sheet. All the fear she had when she first set out came back to her.

When she reached the edge of the broken ice, three men were waiting. One was holding a coil of rope, another a gaff. "Where's Jimmy to?" asked a bearded man, the eldest of the three. There was no mistaking the concern in his voice.

Katie explained who she was and that Jimmy would be by tomorrow with the nurse.

"I'm John Wells," the man said. "And these here is me b'ys, Walter and Earle. We been waitin' since after dinner in case the nurse came this way."

By this time, a group of people had gathered on the ice. Some of the women had blankets under their arms.

"Ye'll have to use th' komatic, Miss," said Earle. "Use it as a bridge to cross over."

Katie looked at the gap in the ice; it must have been at least sixteen feet wide. The komatic was eighteen feet—long enough to fit across the gap, but barely. A wave of panic washed over her. Surely they didn't expect her to walk across on the komatic. She knew how thin ice could get at the edges, and to walk cross over on the sled would be suicide. But what choice did she have? She couldn't go back over the ice.

"We'll t'row yeh a rope, Miss," said Earle. "Tie it to the komatic, then t'row it back to us."

Katie looked again at the wide gap, fear gripping her stomach. One by one, she freed the dogs. One of the men threw her a rope that she tied to the end of the komatic. He pulled and tugged until it lay across the gap like a bridge.

Katie took supplies and medicine from the komatic box and stuffed it into the pocket of her parka. Taking a deep breath, she stepped up on the sled, her legs threatening to buckle. She could feel her heart thudding against her ribs. Carefully, she put one foot in front of the other, taking care not to look down at the black water beneath her.

"You're doin' just fine, Miss Andrews," Earle called as Katie took another stiff step forward.

She tried not to think how thin the ice was at the edges, or that the komatic could go under at any time.

"Only a few more steps now," one of the men said encouragingly.

Katie's breath was coming in sharp, harsh rasps. A cold wind blew in from the north, stinging her face and eyes. She could feel the black water churning beneath her. Panic rose in her throat.

"Jump," John shouted, and Katie made a leap

toward shore. The ice cracked ominously. She could feel the komatic slipping. For a fleeing moment, she caught a glimpse of the panic-stricken faces of the people on the ice.

Water soaked her clothing, filling her boots, causing her legs to go numb.

She was shaking all over. Already her pant legs were starting to freeze. A woman wrapped a blanket around her shoulders; another put a thermos of hot tea to her lips.

Within minutes, the men had the komatic fished out of the water. They harnessed the dogs, and Katie got on the sled while one of the men drove. Halfway up a hill, she felt something nuzzle her neck. "Dodger? Some traveller you are," she laughed scornfully.

A short time later, the driver pulled into the yard of a big house. They were greeted by a young man who helped Katie off the komatic. She followed him inside, wasting no time on idle conversation. He led her through a cheerful kitchen and down a narrow hallway to the sick room.

The little girl in the big bed was flushed with fever, but her eyes were clear. She smiled at Katie when she entered the room.

Katie held out her arms.

A Short History of the Grenfell Mission

*I*n 1892 Wilfred Grenfell, a young doctor recruited by the Royal National Mission to Deep Sea Fishermen, sailed to Labrador on the hospital ship *Albert*. At that time, Labrador was known as the greatest cod fishing ground in the world. Each season, from May to October, as many as 30,000 fishermen and their families sailed there from Newfoundland. Joined by more than 3,000 "livyers" who lived on the coast permanently, they settled in temporary homes in the many isolated inlets, tickles, and bays indenting the coastline.

The fishermen were slaves to a mercantile system that bought their fish and sold them supplies while setting the price for both. Sometimes, after a season of backbreaking work, they would find themselves deeper in debt than when they started out. While in seasons when the fishing was poor the merchants could stand to lose a great deal, more often they became wealthy. At the time of Grenfell's arrival, there was not a single doctor along that stretch of coast. That first season, he traveled more than 2,500 miles in his small launch, visiting 87 settlements and treating 794 patients. He was so moved by the plight of the people and the poverty imposed on them by the system that he dedicated the rest of his life to their service.

Two years after his arrival, he had built a small hospital at Battle Harbour and another at Indian Harbour. Year after year, more projects followed, including more hospitals, cooperatives, nursing stations, schools, and orphanages.

In 1912, Grenfell broke away from the RMDSF, and founded the International Grenfell Association (IGA). By this time, he was so famous his work had become a movement. Most of his time was now spent speaking, fundraising, touring, and recruiting staff to support his work. Skilled professionals came from all over the world to volunteer and work at the mission. International Grenfell Associations sprang up in countries around the world including England, Ireland, Boston, St. John's, and Ottawa.

After his death in 1940, these associations and their branches carried out his work for many years. It wasn't until April 1981, nearly a hundred years after his first visit to the coast, that the IGA was transformed to the Grenfell Regional Health Services Board.

Alice Walsh was born in northern Newfoundland and now lives in Lower Sackville, Nova Scotia. She is the author of four previous books for children, including *Pomiuk: Prince of the North,* which won the 2005 Anne Connor Brimer Award. Alice Walsh holds a Master's degree in Children's Literature from Acadia University.